MW00426718

The Long Italian Goodbye

The Long Italian Goodbye

by

Robert Benedetti

Printed in the United States of America.

For information address:
Durban House Publishing Company, Inc.
7502 Greenville Avenue, Suite 500, Dallas, Texas 75231

Library of Congress Cataloging-in-Publication Data
Robert Benedetti, 1939 –

The Long Italian Goodbye / Robert Benedetti

Library of Congress Control Number: 2004115675

p. cm.

ISBN 1-930754-66-3

First Edition

10 9 8 7 6 5 4 3 2 1

Visit our Web site at
http://www.durbanhouse.com

For Lola and Dino
and the old neighborhood
just off Oakley

PREFACE

A few years ago, I began to notice a big hole inside me where home used to be. Somehow, the old neighborhood, that place where everyone was family, had drifted away. When I looked for it in the real world, I couldn't find it. So I decided to try to write it back into existence.

I started a sort of archeological dig in my memory and began to unearth my old Chicago neighborhood just off Oakley Avenue in 1948. When enough had been uncovered, it began to live again, and to take on a life of its own. Soon things began to happen there, things that hadn't really happened but might have. People appeared, people that hadn't been there before, but now seemed to have been there all along. So although it is inspired by real events, places, and people, this is finally a work of fiction.

For helping me to clear away the rubble of my mind, thanks to Martin Malles. For her generous heart and active assistance, thanks to that wonderful writer, Adriana Trigiani. For his encouragement, thanks to another splendid writer, Ernest Gaines. For believing in my work, thanks to John Lewis and Bob Middlemiss of Durban House. For putting up with me and for many rounds of editing, thanks to my wife Joan. Most of all, love and thanks to my parents and relatives and my extended family in the old neighborhood. They are cherished, and missed beyond words.

Robert Benedetti
Santa Monica, California
January, 2005

1 WINTER MORNING - 1948

He lay perfectly still, feeling his mother's kiss on his cheek and remembering the warmth of her breath as she had bent over him to say goodbye. He let things come into focus, the small plaster medallion in the center of the ceiling, white against pink. He listened for a time to the morning sounds, the low rumble of the furnace on the other side of the wall and the hiss of the steam radiators. Upstairs in his grandparents' flat, a toilet flushed and the water gurgled down the pipe in the wall beside his head. In the gangway outside the kitchen window, the rattle of bottles in the milkman's rack came and went, as reliable as the alarm clock.

Joey threw back the covers and sat up, getting used to the chilly air. He looked over at Clippo, the clown marionette he had gotten for his tenth birthday. Clippo hung with his brilliant white porcelain face looking up at him quizzically, one arm raised in greeting, his red polka dot body dangling from the strings looped over the doorknob.

Good morning, Clippo, Joey said softly.

Good morning, kid, Clippo answered in Joey's voice.

Still in his flannel pajamas, Joey went into the kitchen, his bare feet damp on the cold linoleum. He went to the window and wiped away the condensation. In the back yard, the month-old snow had a dirty crust and the night sky was giving way to a timid dawn. From upstairs came the shuffle of his Nonna's slippers, the running of water, and then the faint scrape of a pot on the stove. Joey went silently down the hall to the front bedroom and put his ear to the door. From inside came his father's muffled snoring.

Joey padded back into the kitchen, quietly opened the back door, and got the milk from the porch. The cold burned his nose, and he opened his mouth and blew out a cloud of steam. Early on every weekday the milkman brought the bottles full of milk with cardboard lids pressed down over the cream that rose up the tapered necks and oozed around the edges. It was one of Joey's chores to put the empty bottles out at night, then as soon as he got up, bring in the fresh milk and put it in the icebox. He closed the back door and put the two fresh bottles of milk on the table. He pried the cardboard lid from one, licked off the cream, and poured some milk into the bowl of Ralston Purina his mother had left for him on the gray Formica top of the chrome kitchen table, then put the bottles in the icebox. As he ate the grainy, tasteless cereal, his eyes traced the maze-like geometric design in the yellow linoleum floor.

When he was done, he rinsed the bowl and spoon, dried them, and put them away in the tiny pantry beside the sink. Right on time, he heard the crunch of the iceman's footsteps coming down the gangway to the back door. Once a week in winter and twice in summer the iceman came, carrying with his iron tongs a glistening block of ice from the refrigerated wagon that stood on the street, its blindered horse standing stoically with its snout buried in a canvas feed sack, munching steadily, occasionally raising its tail and dropping a great gob of steaming manure onto the dirty snow. The iceman knew not to knock for fear of awakening Father, and Joey hurried to open the door. The iceman was burly, with a wild beard, a flat cap, and a heavy flannel shirt bulging out of his denim overalls. His eyebrows were so bushy Joey could barely make out the glint of his dark eyes. He entered without so much as a glance in Joey's direction and hefted the block into the sink. Joey marveled at the man's skill as he cut the block with only one or two jabs of his pick until it exactly fit the metal-lined compartment in the top of the icebox. Then he sheathed his pick and, still without speaking, turned and left, dropping the excess pieces of ice into the snow outside the back door.

Joey went back into his bedroom to dress. His mother had laid out his clothes and Joey's heart sank when he saw the woolen pants. His parents had bought them at the employee sale of unclaimed alterations at the Hart, Schaffner and Marx factory where his mother's mother, Nonna Severina, made buttonholes by hand. Joey hated wool. It made his skin itch. When the pants were brought home, Joey had refused to wear them, but his father made him put them on. At first Joey walked stiff-legged so they wouldn't touch his skin. His father was infuriated at the waste of a good pair of pants and had insisted that he walk right in them, but his mother intervened and a compromise had been reached. Joey was now allowed to wear his flannel pajama bottoms under the hated pants.

When he had smoothed the pajamas under the pants and had pulled on his shirt, he tucked his doubled-over pants inside his black galoshes, drew the fastenings closed and snapped them shut. He wrapped his muffler around his neck, put on his knitted cap, slid on his bulky corduroy coat, and pulled up the knitted mittens his mother had long ago attached to his coat by a humiliating string that ran up one sleeve and down the other. He took his bag lunch out of the icebox and quietly passed through the back door, locking it after him. He took a deep breath of the cold air. He had a special feeling about this day, though he couldn't think why. He set off, ready for whatever might come.

Joey went through his own backyard, past the dried stalks of last summer's hollyhocks that stuck up through the snow, and up the three steps to the alley gate. He always took this shortcut to school, going through the alley that ran along a big empty lot all the way to Cermak Road. Joey walked in the ruts made by the few cars that were kept in the garages that lined the alley, past the wooden fences that ran along one side. In the middle of the lot, opposite the fences, was a little hill where, after a snowfall, his father sometimes took him sledding on his prized Radio Flyer.

This morning there was a group of older boys huddled around a puddle of icy water at the base of the hill. Joey looked over their shoulders and saw Rex, an eighth-grader, at the center of the circle. As befitted his name, Rex was big and strong, with a bristly crew cut and a square jaw. He was the acknowledged leader of the gang of big boys who enjoyed tormenting Joey. There was Primo, Rex's second-in-command, and his younger brother Secundo, and Louis Baldi, a fourth cousin of Joey's, and Perry Anzilotti, the nephew of the neighborhood funeral parlor owner, and Alphonse Zanardo, whom everybody called Capone because of his first name.

Rex had a burlap sack from which came the sound of frantic mewing. He reached into the sack and took out a little kitten, just born, its eyes not yet open.

Watch this, he said. He put the kitten into the puddle and held it under the muddy water until little bubbles came up. The circle of crouching boys stared in fascination until the kitten stopped moving, and Rex withdrew the limp body and held it out to them in the palm of his hand.

Wow, said one of the boys, I never saw nothing die before. Rex looked up at Joey and saw the horror in his eyes. He reached into the bag and withdrew another kitten, and held it out, wriggling, toward Joey.

Here, kid, he said, you do one. Joey shrank back. What's the matter, Rex said, you chicken? Joey turned and ran up the hill, slipping frantically on the icy snow. Rex yelled, Look at the little chicken run! and the other boys howled. When Joey looked back, he saw them huddled again intently over the puddle.

Joey felt dizzy and sick to his stomach. He walked as if in a trance the half block to the crossing at the corner of Cermak Road and Oakley Avenue. He straightened up when he saw his cousins, Benita Fantozzi and her brother Peter, waiting. The Fantozzi house was the fanciest house on Twenty-Second Place, right at the corner of Oakley Avenue, a house of yellow pressed brick that stood out from all the other darker, plain brick houses. Old man Fantozzi, known simply as Fan, was the neighborhood insurance broker, but during the Depression had forgiven so many premiums and had lent so much money to those in need that he had become a sort of bank for the neighborhood after the real banks had failed. He was trusted without reservation by everyone and soon became an alderman, a beneficent elder who, it was said, had the ear of the mayor. He sat every day behind his polished wood desk in his handsome mahogany-paneled office on Oakley Avenue, smoking small pungent Italian cigars. Fan dispensed insurance and advice, settled disputes and the estates of the dearly departed, got garbage collected and water turned back on. The neighborhood had no need of a Mafia Godfather, Joey's father used to say, they had Fan.

Fan's two children glowed in the reflected light of their father's reputation, Peter being considered the smartest boy in the sixth grade, and Benita, with her curly golden hair, the prettiest girl. The Fantozzis were the neighborhood aristocrats, and although they were distant cousins of Joey's, Joey's family were decidedly serfs. Nevertheless, Joey felt familial pride in their kinship, though if you went back far enough, almost everyone in the neighborhood was related to everyone else in some way.

Hi, they all said to one another, it sure is cold, my mom says it'll get warmer soon, there isn't going to be any more snow, not for a while anyway, we've had enough already, I'm already sick of it.

Joey felt a special connection with Benita, partly because they were both a little chubby, but mostly because they had both been skipped ahead a grade and were now the two youngest kids in sixth grade, though Joey thought of Benita as older. His mother said that girls matured faster than boys, and Joey guessed that this was true; Benita certainly seemed less bewildered by life than he was. Joey thought about how his mother had said they were kissing cousins. He wondered if Benita liked him, but would never dare ask. Mostly, he assumed that he was invisible to her.

The three of them waited together on the corner behind Big Paulie, who lived three doors down from Joey and was the biggest kid in the sixth grade by any measurement. He was the crossing guard at this, the most prestigious corner, with a white Sam Browne belt over his coat and a miniature red stop sign that he held like a ping-pong paddle. Although Big Paulie was a year older than Joey, they were chums, and in most things Big Paulie followed Joey's lead. Here, however, Big Paulie was bolstered by his authority and uniform, and ran his corner with military precision.

A streetcar went by, a conductor bundled in his coat on the rear platform, ringing his bell. Peter gathered up a handful of wet snow and threw it at the conductor, who shook his fist at them.

Big Paulie said, Hey, cut that out or I'll report you.

Benita said, Peter, you're going to get into trouble.

Peter said, Hell, I missed him anyway. Big Paulie went out into the street and, even though there were no cars coming, stood at attention with one hand up holding the little stop sign, the other arm stretched out to the side, beckoning them to cross, looking courageous.

As they passed him Benita lowered her eyes and said, Thank you Paul, and Joey felt his heart sink. Hell, he thought, someday I'll be a damn crossing guard.

On the other side of Cermak Road Joey helped Benita over the ridge that the snowplow had made, now melted into a wet, icy mound. The kids all said that Cermak Road was named for a mayor of Chicago who was shot just down the street by the Mafia while riding in a car next to FDR during a parade, and nobody knew if it was just a mistake and if FDR had been the real target, or whether Al Capone had ordered the killing from prison just to show FDR that he could kill anyone he wanted to, any time he wanted to. The West Side had been one of Capone's neighborhoods, and there was always an echo of pride in the telling of this story.

The playground at Pickard School was large and noisy and full of children. Joey was hanging from one of the monkey bars when suddenly he felt something like an electric shock and everything went black and silent. He fell into a heap, groping in the darkness. What was happening? He pulled off a mitten and touched his face, but it was numb. Oh God, he thought, maybe I had a stroke and will have to ride in a wheelchair and have somebody feed me like Great-Uncle Caesar. Full of apprehension, he tried to wiggle his toes.

When he had fallen off his bike once his mother had made him wiggle his toes, and had said, Thank God, your legs aren't broken. Thank God, they wiggled. Gradually, his vision and hearing returned. His face started to burn. He wiped ice crystals out of his nose and eyes. He heard laughter, and looked up. He saw Rex doubled over, laughing at him. Primo had thrown the snowball and was receiving the congratulations of Secundo, Capone, and the rest of the gang.

Benita was holding Joey by the arm, yelling, You okay? He hit you with an iceball right in the face, and I think your nose is bleeding. Joey dabbed at his nose and saw a bit of blood.

Peter said, I bet that bastard put a rock inside it.

Joey felt his breath coming in little spurts, his heart pounding. He got shakily to his feet and staggered toward Primo, his teeth and fists clenched, screaming, *Figlio di una cagna! Bastardo*! Primo and the gang laughed all the more. Then Joey was on him, flailing wildly.

A great cry went up, Fight! Fight! All the kids crowded around while Joey and Primo struggled. In their bulky winter coats, neither boy had much effect on the other, but they beat at each other for all they were worth.

Get the little runt, Rex was yelling.

Benita was yelling for Joey to get Primo good, hit him, hit him.

Peter and several other boys finally managed to drag Joey off, yelling, A teacher's gonna come, you better stop it. Just as Peter pulled Joey away, Primo landed a solid punch on Joey's nose. Joey fell to his knees and the blood spurted out in earnest.

Somebody said, Here comes Mrs. Schlagle, and the crowd ran and Primo, Secundo, Rex, and the rest of the gang melted away. Only Benita stayed at Joey's side.

Mrs. Schlagle, Joey's feared sixth grade teacher, was the playground monitor. She marched up to Joey and Benita and demanded, What's going on here?

Joey stammered, Nothing, Mrs. Schlagle.

Benita started to say, Primo hit him, but Joey cut her off, saying, It's nothing, I just sneezed and got a bloody nose. Joey looked darkly at Benita, his eyes reminding her that no matter what, kids always banded together against the teachers, and they never, never snitched.

Mrs. Schlagle walked away, saying, Hold some snow against your nose, it'll stop. It's almost time for the first bell.

Benita led Joey away and sat him down on a bench. She took some snow in her hand and held it against Joey's nose, and said, You should have told. Joey shook his head. He looked up and saw the other kids watching them sitting together on the bench, Benita with one arm around his shoulder, holding snow against his nose. The girls especially had sly smiles.

Joey suddenly got up and said, That's okay, I'll be fine, and moved away, holding the wad of snow against his nose, his face burning, though not from the cold.

The first bell rang, and the children lined up according to their grades. They stomped their feet to stay warm and a few more snowballs were thrown when Mrs. Schlagle wasn't looking. Then the second bell rang and the teachers opened the doors and the lines marched into the school in order. There was an upright piano on the landing of the main stairwell and the music teacher, Mrs. Anderson, played a rousing march while an older student beat time on a snare drum. Everyone marched single-file, keeping to the right side of the hallways and stairs, lines moving in both directions at once. When the sixth graders arrived at room 103, Joey and the others went first into the cloakroom and hung up their hats and coats and mittens and took off their galoshes and rubbers and piled them helter-skelter. The cloakroom was always the scene of surreptitious jabbing and practical jokes. Benita moved close to Joey and whispered, I hope your nose is okay, I thought you were very brave. Joey felt her warm breath on his cheek, which still burned, and his breath caught.

Sure, it's fine, thanks, Joey said, and hurried to his seat.

The sixth grade had about twenty kids in it, and was ruled with an iron fist by Mrs. Schlagle. She allowed no one to speak until they had raised their hand and been called upon. Around eleven o'clock, as they were taking turns standing in front of the class reading the day's lesson aloud, Joey had a powerful urge to pee. He raised his hand, but Mrs. Schlagle refused to interrupt Benita, who was reading a passage about the Bill of Rights. He lowered his hand and tried to suppress the urge, but soon his bladder felt like it would burst. He waved his hand again desperately. Angrily, Mrs. Schlagle told him to put his hand down until they were done with the exercise. Soon there was no holding back, and Joey felt the warm wetness running down his leg. Looking down, he was horrified to see a yellow puddle forming on the wooden floor beneath his desk. With his foot, he tried to push it squeegee-like under the desk in front of him, hoping that the blame would fall on poor, unsuspecting Walter Siroka, who sat there. Walter had a tremendously long face, and pointy teeth with big spaces between them. He stuck out his tongue when he talked and it had strange craters in it, as if punctured by his pointed teeth. Joey felt a strong, irrational sympathy for Walter Siroka and imagined all sorts of terrible things about Walter's home life, but at this moment Joey was willing to sacrifice him.

Lenora Gonzini, who sat next to Joey, noticed what he was doing and started to giggle. Mrs. Schlagle was there in a shot. She looked down and saw the puddle of urine and the muscles of her jaw tightened. Without a word, she took Joey by the ear and marched him out of the room into the main hallway, where there was a huge iron grate in the floor from which heat rose from the furnace below. Mrs. Schlagle placed Joey over the grate and ordered him to stand there, legs apart, until his pants dried. Then she disappeared down the stairs. Standing there, Joey glanced at the classroom door, where he could see Walter Siroka peeking out at him through the window, holding his hand across his mouth, his eyes crinkled in glee. Walter disappeared as Mrs. Schlagle marched back up the stairs and went into the classroom without speaking or looking at Joey. A few minutes later, the janitor, a tall, thin black man with a mustache in baggy overalls, trudged up the stairs with his mop and bucket. He looked grimly down at Joey and shook his head, then went into the classroom.

Joey stood over the grate being washed in the waves of hot air that floated up. The wet pajamas under his pants could no longer protect him from the wool, and the itching grew worse with each passing minute. It was all he could do to stop himself from tearing the pants off. The janitor came out of the classroom and trudged back downstairs with his mop and bucket. An eternity passed. Joey could see that the stain was still clearly visible, the thickness of the flannel pajamas inside the wool pants holding the wetness like a diaper. Then, to his horror, Mrs. Anderson and the drummer appeared and took their places on the main stair landing above him. The class-changing bell rang and Mrs. Anderson began to play "The Double Eagle March." The classroom doors burst open and lines of children came out and marched past Joey on their way to lunch. Walter Siroka snickered as he went by, but Benita hit him in the back and said, Shush! Joey met her eyes, which were filled with a deep sympathy that made Joey shrivel inside. He stood there, staring at the ground, in nothing but shame, listening to the giggles of the passing children. Then he remembered the cries and bubbles of the drowning kittens, and for the first time in his life took comfort from the thought that things could always be worse.

Once everyone had filed past, Mrs. Schlagle cut Joey down from his cross. Though his pants looked dry, the flannel pajama liner was still damp, and he knew he would itch and smell for the rest of the day. He got his bag lunch and went to room 207 where, every Monday, he and nine other kids whose parents paid an extra fifty cents a semester spent their lunch hour at a piano lesson. Joey sat in the back, away from the eyes and noses of the other kids. He quickly ate his bologna sandwich, mayonnaise only, with its wilted lettuce. He drank his carton of chocolate milk and chewed his two vanilla wafers. The wafers always comforted him. They reminded him of the fine malted milks at the Rexall drug store on Cermak Road with its marble counter, shiny chrome stools, gracefully arched soda taps with the black bakelite handles that dispensed bubbly soda water when turned one way, and a thin, hard stream when turned the other, and the malts that came in tall fluted glasses with a second helping in the metal can, so thick the straw collapsed when you sucked on it, and always accompanied by two vanilla wafers.

Joey was lost in this reverie when Mrs. Anderson said, If everyone is done eating, let's begin. Joey and the other kids opened their desks and took out their keyboards, cardboard strips with piano keys printed on them, which they unfolded and laid across their desks. Pickard School had only two real pianos, the one on the landing, and the other in this room. The kids took turns, one each week, playing the real piano, while the rest of the class played along on their cardboard keyboards, the quiet thumping of their fingers keeping time with the metronome on Mrs. Anderson's desk. This morning they thumped out "Three Blind Mice" while poor Walter Siroka, his cratered tongue sticking out in fevered concentration, tried to hit a few right notes on the real piano.

Joey was thankful that he had not yet been called on to play the piano up in front. His Nonna Augusta had an upright piano in her parlor upstairs on which Joey was supposed to practice. Unfortunately it was a player piano, and in the attic he had discovered a big trunk full of piano rolls, mostly arias from operas with the Italian lyrics printed on them so that they appeared in a little window on the front of the piano as the roll moved past. It was so much fun to pump the pedals and make the piano play, experimenting with the controls that changed the tempo and dynamics, that there seemed no point in learning to play himself. Instead, Joey dreamed of being an orchestra conductor. When he was alone in the house, he would often put a 78 rpm record on his folks' big Capehart-Farnsworth console and pretend that he was conducting the orchestra and singers in the Quartet from *Rigoletto* or the Sextette from *Lucia*, waving his arms as he had once seen Arturo Toscanini do in a newsreel.

When the bell rang at the end of the piano lesson, Joey folded his cardboard keyboard and heard Mrs. Anderson announce that for next week everyone should practice "Twinkle, Twinkle, Little Star." And then the dreaded words, Joey, you'll be the player.

Joey marched like a condemned man to his afternoon classroom, considering what illness might keep him home from school Monday and wondering what further humiliations Pickard School might have in store for him.

2

RUNNING COFFEE

THANKFULLY, JOEY'S AFTERNOON CLASS PASSED WITHOUT INCIDENT. He survived by avoiding eye contact with anyone, especially Benita. Fifteen minutes before the dismissal bell, everyone marched back to their homerooms, Mrs. Anderson and the drummer regaling them with "The March of the Toreadors" from *Carmen*. The march reopened the wound of Joey's lunchtime pillory and there were waves of barely suppressed hilarity in the ranks.

At last back in his homeroom downstairs, Joey kept his eyes in a book, scanning the words without really seeing them, glancing up at the hands of the big round clock on the wall as they ticked their way toward three o'clock. When the alarm bell in the hallway jangled, everyone packed up their things, slammed their desks shut, and rushed to the cloakroom. Elbowing for position, they pulled on their galoshes, wound themselves into their mufflers, and wormed into their bulky winter coats. Many sported bright new hand-knitted mittens or scarves, three-week-old Christmas presents. The shock of returning to school after the holiday had already worn off and the freedom of the impending weekend was as welcome as ever.

Joey was hurrying across the playground, eager to get away from the whispered conversations, real and imagined, that followed in his wake. A familiar voice called, Hey, Joey, wait up! It was Big Paulie. Joey took refuge under the monkey bars as he caught up. Big Paulie seemed incapable of speaking softly and his voice was so much like a donkey's bray that some called him Jackass, and his own family called him *Chiaccierone*, loudmouth. Big Paulie said, in a voice that could be heard a block away, I guess you had a little accident this morning. Several passing kids laughed, and Joey sucked in his chin and thought that if anyone at Pickard School had not yet heard about it, they knew now.

Joey said, I'd rather not talk about it.

Sure, I know how you must feel, I just wondered if you still wanted to go treasure hunting?

Might as well, Joey said without enthusiasm.

Big Paulie fell into a sympathetic silence. He was a crossing guard only in the mornings, and after school he and Joey always took a secret detour on their way home.

The two boys stood quietly while the playground emptied. Benita and a group of girls were the last to pass through the gate onto Cermak Road. Lenora Gonzini looked back at Joey and said something to the others, holding her hand in front of her mouth. The others glanced surreptitiously at Joey and giggled, but Benita spoke sharply, a stern look on her face, and the others quickly fell silent and hurried on their way. When the girls got to the corner of Oakley Avenue, Benita glanced back in Joey's direction and gave him a sad smile.

Gee, Big Paulie said, I think she likes you.

Joey could feel his face redden. Don't be crazy, he said aloud, though his breath caught and his heart was pounding.

The boys lingered until everyone was well out of sight, then ducked around the corner of the school and stepped into the gloom of the narrow brick-walled gorge that ran between the school and the factory next door. They sloshed through the melting snow in the alley, their footsteps showing black through the icy crust. The factory did something called electroplating, making shiny metal parts for appliances and toys. The garbage cans in the alley often held defective parts in fantastic shapes that were discarded about this time every afternoon. Joey and Big Paulie came right after school to have first picks, and had kept the source of their treasure secret ever since Joey had discovered it last Halloween. They walked carefully, without speaking, for there was an old black security guard who had once run them off when he caught them rummaging in the cans. They approached the first of the large metal cans and peered in. Among the dull castings gleamed something special.

Hold on to me, Big Paulie whispered, and Joey grabbed the bigger boy's belt. Big Paulie disappeared up to his waist in the can, his feet dangling skyward. After a moment his muffled voice floated up. Wow, look at this one! Joey pulled and Big Paulie came up waving a large shiny casting like a ray gun, Zap! Zap!

Hey, you boys there! A deep voice echoed between the brick walls of the alley, hitting the two boys like an electric shock.

We're gonna get arrested, Big Paulie yelled and tried to throw the part back in the can, but the frigid metal stuck to his wet gloves. He turned and ran for all he was worth, dropping his glove with the ray gun stuck to it in the snow. Joey started to follow, but slipped on a patch of ice under the dirty slush. He fell on his knees, tried to catch himself with his mittened hands, but felt the icy water pour into the top of his rubber galoshes.

As he scrambled to get up, the voice called again, It's okay, okay, I just want to ask you something.

Joey stopped, his heart pounding, pumping out puffs of steam. He turned warily and asked, What?

The voice called, Come here, by the window, I ain't gonna hurt you.

The voice seemed to come from one of the windows a short way up the alley. Joey approached slowly, his feet growing numb from the water in his boots. He reached up on tiptoe and peered in. The window was set behind a row of rusty iron bars, and the glass, so dirty it might as well have been painted black, had a crisscrossed web of metal wires running through it. The center pane was tilted open, and it was through this opening that the voice came, the dialect so thick Joey could barely understand what the man was saying.

We needs you to go get some coffee for us. We ain't allowed to go outside, and there ain't no coffee in here. We'll pay you a nickel to get it.

Joey considered this a moment. As his eyes adjusted to the darkness behind the window, he could make out the face of a black man. He was not brown like some Negroes Joey had seen, but a deep blue-black. There was a whir of machinery behind the man, and a whiff of acrid air came out of the window and made Joey's eyes sting. Joey said, Okay, how many?

The man said, We wants five, two black, three white. Here, here's the money. The man reached out through the bars and opened his hand, offering some coins. Joey was surprised to see that the black hand had a white palm, crossed by dark creases like veins in a leaf. The man said, We gonna trust you not to run off with it and if'n you do we gonna find you and whup you upside the head, you hear?

Joey said, Sure, and took the money.

The coffee shop was just around the corner and a block down Western Avenue. As Joey turned the corner, the cold January wind blew grit into his eyes. He wound his muffler around his mouth and over his nose. His shoes and socks were wet through, but the water in his galoshes had warmed, and he made a loud sloshing sound as he trudged along the partly shoveled sidewalk. Western was a big street, the brick pavement pushed into a series of grooves and bumps by the heavy trucks that rumbled by. In the center of the street, two shiny tracks were embedded into the bricks, and just now two streetcars passed each other going in opposite directions, their long, raised wands whistling as they ran on the overhead electric wires, sparking when they crossed a junction.

By the time Joey got to the coffee shop, crystals of ice were forming where his breath hit his muffler. Opening the door and stepping inside, the humid heat of the shop hit him like a wall. A few men sitting on low stools at the cracked and peeling green linoleum counter turned to peer at this outsider. Behind the counter was a big woman with frizzy gray hair that had once been blond. Joey pulled his muffler down, now soaked where the ice crystals had melted, and said, I want some coffee, please.

The woman looked down at him and smiled, Well, they start drinking coffee young around here. A large man sitting at the end of the counter laughed, a raspy, grating laugh like two pieces of rusty metal being scraped together.

No, Ma'am, Joey said, it ain't for me, it's for the workers in the factory.

The man snorted, He's runnin' coffee for the niggers.

The large woman frowned at the man and said, You hush, at least they's got jobs. She turned to Joey and said, How many?

Joey repeated the order, Two black, three white.

The lady said, To go is extra, I got to charge you an extra two cents for the paper cups.

That's okay, ma'am. As she poured the coffee, Joey did some arithmetic in his head. The extra two cents for each of the five coffees meant ten cents more. He sorted through the coins the man had given him. Even with the five cents he was being paid, he was five cents short. Ma'am, he said, I don't have enough.

She looked back at him over her shoulder. How much you missin'?

Five cents, Joey said, I'm sorry.

Well, the lady said, taking the coins from him, you just bring it next time. She put the five paper cups full of coffee on the counter and snapped cardboard lids into them. Joey tried to gather them up but the woman said, You gonna spill those sure. Here, I got a box lid you can put 'em in.

As Joey started carefully back down Western holding the box lid, he began to form a plan. Running coffee, the man had said. Two cents extra for each paper cup. Joey stopped as the idea came into focus. He walked back to the coffee shop and pushed open the door, stuck in his head and asked, What if I brought my own cups or something, would you still need to charge me the extra two cents?

The woman looked up and said, No, I fill thermoses for the men all the time, no extra charge. And close the door, it's freezing out there!

Joey squished quickly back to the factory window. As he handed in the cups, he explained that the coffee had been twelve cents instead of ten.

Shit, the man said, two cents for a paper cup, that's highway robbery. But he handed out an extra dime.

Maybe, Joey said, I could fill your thermoses for you.

The man laughed. We ain't got no thermoses, what do you think we is, Rockefellers?

Joey said he would try to figure something out.

As he walked home he puzzled over the problem. He knew he could not ask his mother or father for help. They would only tell him not to have anything to do with the black workers. Big Paulie and the other kids would want to horn in on his business. There was only one other person he trusted enough to ask, and that was his godfather, Bruno Gini, a sixteen-year-old third cousin who lived across the street. But Joey decided against it. He was driven by an urge to do this on his own, seized for the first time by the dream of self-sufficiency, of earning an independent income that might rescue him from serfdom and elevate him in the hierarchy of the neighborhood a step or two closer to the level of Benita Fantozzi. But first he had to find a way to transport the coffee.

As he always did, he took the short cut home through the empty lot behind his house, past the place of execution, following the wheel ruts in the alley leading to his back gate. It was here that fate intervened. As he opened the gate, a lone ray of sunlight broke through the clouds and fell upon a discarded wire milk bottle basket, like the one their own milkman used, sticking up through the snow. It was badly bent, but it glowed with possibility, and it inspired in Joey a wonderful plan. Like the young Arthur pulling Excalibur out of the stone, Joey pulled the rack out of the snow and carried it to his back door.

As usual, Joey was more or less on his own for an hour or two after school. His mother left for work at seven every morning, since it took her an hour to travel by streetcar to her accounting job at the Samsonite suitcase factory. His father worked the graveyard shift at

International Harvester, so he was asleep when Joey left for school in the morning, and went to work just before Joey got home. His father's mother, Nonna Augusta, who lived upstairs, watched Joey after school until his mother got home from work at six. Joey was expected to report to Nonna immediately after school, but in practice he had considerable leeway thanks to his grandmother's vague sense of time, which she had acquired growing up on a farm in Italy where time was measured by the angle of the sun and not by the hands of the clock.

Joey used his key to quietly enter the basement flat where he and his parents lived. He pulled open the drawer in which his father kept a few tools and took out a hammer and pliers. Outside the back door he cleared enough snow from the pavement to pound and bend the wire rack until it was more or less straight. Then he hid it in the cupboard under the back stairs.

That night after dinner, he went out on the pretense of seeing some friend or other. Under cover of darkness, he crept through the backyards of the neighboring houses. On most of the porches, empty milk bottles were already set out. When there were several empties on a porch, Joey took one, hoping that its absence would not be noticed. He hid the empty bottles in the rack in the cupboard until he had a dozen. So eager was he to begin earning the money that would make him worthy of Benita that he determined to forgo an illness and brave even the dreaded piano lesson on Monday. He practiced all Saturday and Sunday afternoon, and was soon able to pick out the melody of "Twinkle, Twinkle, Little Star" over two block chords in the left hand.

And so, the following Monday morning, he was ready to begin running coffee.

3

BOOKER T

MONDAY MORNING DAWNED COLD AND CRISP. Joey had hardly slept, and when his mother came in to kiss him goodbye, he kept his eyes closed and pretended to be asleep. He waited for her footsteps in the gangway to die away, then got up, brought in the milk, had a hurried breakfast, dressed, and closed the door quietly when he went out.

The floor of the back porch creaked as he crept to the cupboard under the stairs that led up to his grandparents' flat. The porch had been enclosed years before by his father and an old carpenter named Matseo who lived up the street. Matseo was not the best of carpenters and all the stair steps he had built were slightly different heights, so people who weren't used to them often stumbled. Joey remembered vividly that Matseo had only a stump where his left thumb should have been. Father said he had sawn it off by mistake.

Joey quietly opened the cupboard door. He moved aside the gardening equipment that screened his hiding place. From the back of the cabinet he lifted out his precious wire basket and the twelve empty milk bottles it held, and put his school lunch in its place. Joey quietly closed the cupboard door and tiptoed across the creaking floor to the outer door of the porch.

As he opened it, he heard a call from above, *Oh Joey, Perché sta andando via così presto?* Why are you leaving so early? Damn! His Nonna Augusta was leaning out the second-floor window of the back porch, pinning freshly washed clothes to the line his father had rigged through a pulley across the yard so the clothes could be high up into the sun. Joey quickly set the basket and bottles down out of sight and stepped into the yard.

He looked up and said*, Io sto incontrando degli amici*. I'm meeting some friends.

Oh, Nonna said, *è a casa prossima per pranzo*? Will you be home for lunch?

He answered, *No, Nonna, oggi è la mia lezione di pianoforte.* Today is my piano lesson.

In the few words of broken English she knew, Nonna called back, her breath billowing in the low sunlight, Hokay, Joey, atsa good. She gave him her usual final benediction, Be car-ie-ful, and closed the window.

When he was sure she was inside, Joey retrieved the bottles. He hurried out toward the front of the house and street, going the way the milkman and iceman went, through a narrow gangway between his house and the next, then up the cement steps with the ornate black iron railing to the street above. His father had explained that years ago the city of Chicago had filled in the streets here, raising them seven feet because the land had once been a marsh. This left all the houses in the neighborhood with basements that had originally been at ground level. There was even an old front door on the lower level that no one used anymore, hidden in shadows underneath the new front steps that reached like a bridge from the raised street to the new front door on the second floor.

Under the sidewalk at the front of the house was a dark space Father said was once a coal bin, now boarded shut for fear of Joey getting in where there might be rats and certainly lots of dirt. Joey usually took a moment to peek through the cracks in the boards into the gloom, where a little filtered light came from the cloudy bulls-eyes of glass set into the iron manhole through which coal had once been delivered, imagining what might lurk in the depths. But this morning he hurried up the stairs without stopping.

Joey started down still-silent Twenty-Second Place, the basket hanging at his side, rattling just like the milkman. The street was only one block long, running from Western Avenue at one end to Oakley Avenue at the other. Though Western was the bigger street, Oakley Avenue was more famous as the heart of the Tuscan neighborhood in which they lived. Everyone here was careful to distinguish this northern Italian neighborhood from the southern Italian neighborhood to the north known as Little Italy. For the Toscanos in Joey's world, the true Italy extended only as far south as Rome, and people whose roots were in Naples or, God forbid, Sicily, might as well have come from another planet. When people asked anyone in Joey's family where they lived in Chicago, they always said proudly, Just off Oakley.

Joey stepped carefully over the patches of icy snow next door. The people who lived there never shoveled their sidewalk. He had glimpsed these neighbors only a few times, shriveled, gray people, who never spoke and stared at the ground when they walked. In the front window of their house was a banner, white satin with vertical red stripes on both sides and four gold stars stacked up the center. It had hung there for three years now, ever since the War had ended, and was faded by the sun. Joey remembered some things about the War, the little Victory Garden his mother had planted in the backyard, the precious books full of rationing stamps, the pennies he had saved for the War Bond drive at school. He dimly remembered the rejoicing of VE day, then later, the newsreel pictures of the huge bomb with its mushroom cloud, then more rejoicing at VJ day. Now, the only visible reminder of the War was this faded banner. Other houses in the neighborhood had once had similar banners, most with one star, a few with two, but they had long since been taken down. Only this one, with its four stars, remained. When Joey asked what it meant, his father said each star stood for a son who had been lost in the War. All four, his father said, and shook his head sadly. He said he hoped that Joey would never have to go away to war like that. Looking at the banner now, Joey understood why the snow was never shoveled on this sidewalk.

The sun was just touching the tops of the buildings as he hurried into the alley behind the factory. Only a glimmer of light was reflected from the sooty bricks of the adjoining school building. He stopped in front of the window, reached through the rusty bars and thumped on the glass with his mittened hand, leaving marks in the grime. After a few moments, the man tilted the center pane open.

Hey, coffee boy, he said with surprise, I didn't think we'd see you again. You figured something out?

Joey lifted the rack into view and said, I got some milk bottles here, and I can bring you coffee in them and you can wash them out when you're through and I'll get them every morning. You don't need to pay me extra, just the two cents for every cup that you'll be saving.

The man laughed, Shit, you got a head on you for sure, be right back.

Joey could hear voices inside and he reached up on tiptoe,

peering in, just able to make out a group of workers in elbow-length black rubber gloves and aprons that covered them to their necks. They were all black men, and Joey thought they looked like phantoms, their eyes and teeth shining in the gloom. Behind them, a few naked light bulbs reflected on pieces of raw metal hanging from chains above long vats of bubbling chemicals throwing up misty vapors that even through the small window stung Joey's nose and made his eyes water.

Soon the man came back and said, Four black, four white, one just sugar, and chocolate milk for the boy.

Sure, Joey said, and repeated the order just to make sure.

The man pulled off his long rubber glove and reached out through the bars, passing Joey a handful of loose change. Joey got another whiff of the acrid air from inside and asked, How can you stand that smell?

Oh, shit, the man said, you get so's you hardly notice it. Now we's got to sneak this coffee down while the boss is gone, so hurry up.

The man turned back to work and as he stepped aside, Joey caught a glimpse of the boy. He was about Joey's height, dressed in overalls and a denim shirt. He had no gloves or apron, but he wore tall rubber boots that were several sizes too big. He was wiping the floor beneath the tanks with a mop. He looked up at Joey, and their eyes met. Joey smiled, but the boy only stared without expression, then went back to his mopping.

Joey took his rack full of bottles and went back up the alley, past the garbage cans, stepping over the narrow river of dark melt water that flowed down the middle of the cracked cement, a rainbow swirl of oil floating on top. Clouds of steam billowed out of vents in the electroplating factory's wall.

Out on the street, he crossed carefully, looking both ways as his mother had told him to do ever since his cousin Flora had been hit by the laundry truck and the Fire Department ambulance had come. At dinner the night of the accident, his father told him that he had, in his youth, been a six-day bicycle racer until Angelino, his boyhood racing partner, had been killed by a UPS truck that backed up and crushed him as he rode by on his racing bike. Joey knew about six-day bicycle races. He had once seen a newsreel of the racers pedaling at terrific speed around the steeply banked wooden track of the velodrome that stood in the city park they sometimes visited by streetcar on Sundays. But it was the first time he had imagined that his father might have done such a thing. And he wondered how even his father could ride a bicycle for six days.

When Joey got to Western Avenue, there were three streetcars backed up at the signal light at Cermak. In the morning chill the streetcar windows were fogged and Joey could see only the shapes of people huddled inside where electric heaters gave a little warmth. One of the cars stopped at the corner as Joey walked past, the wheels grating on the sand that poured onto the track from bins hung on the front of the cars during winter. An old black woman wearing galoshes just like his got off and shuffled through the slush toward the factory. Joey knew that black people lived far away on the south side of the city, and he realized the men and boy in the factory had to travel even further than his mother to get to work.

Joey hurried past the Sinclair gas station on the corner, past the big green pumps with round white illuminated tops and a green dinosaur on the sign. This was where his father took their Packard to get gas and fill the tires. Father had told him how, during the Depression, he and his friends would pull into this station at night and empty the gas out of the hoses into their cars, collecting just enough to take their girls for a ride. When Father told this story, Joey's mother laughed and said, Yes, and how often we ran out of gas and had to walk home!

Father remembered how hard it had been for them to be alone together when they were courting, their folks insisting they always have a chaperone or go out in a group. Mother shook her head and said, I don't know what they thought we would do if we were ever alone for a few minutes.

Father laughed. I do, and they were right.

Oh, Dino, really!

Joey tried to imagine his mother as a young girl with his father as a young man, and what they might have done if they had been alone for a few minutes, but the image was disturbing and he pushed it away.

In the coffee shop, the big woman with the frizzy hair smiled when Joey came in and said, So, you come back, and how are you this morning, young man?

I'm fine, Joey said, and he put the rack and bottles on the counter. Can I get coffee in these?

Sure, ain't you a smart one.

Joey repeated the order from memory, four black, four white, one just sugar, and one chocolate milk.

The same large man was sitting at the end of the counter and said, So you goin' into business, are you?

Joey said, Yes sir, I am, you kinda gave me the idea, running coffee you said.

Well I'll be damned, the man said, and stirred his coffee.

The woman laughed, See, the boy's got get up and go, he ain't gonna sit around on his backside and collect unemployment all his life like some.

The man snorted and said, High talk from somebody who slings coffee.

She snorted back, I didn't always do this, there's lots about me you don't know.

The woman gathered up the bottles, clutching them to the dirty white apron tied around her huge waist. It's already after eight, she said, you gonna be late for school.

Joey shook his head. I got plenty of time to deliver the coffee and still get to school before the bell at eight thirty.

Well, you better have a bite against the cold. She lifted the round plastic cover from the plate of doughnuts on the counter and pushed it toward him.

Joey said, Thank you very much. He took a dark jelly doughnut he hoped would have cream filling inside. The woman took the bottles out of the rack and began filling them from the row of huge, gleaming coffee urns behind the counter. Joey bit into the doughnut, rejoicing that it did in fact have a cream filling. He chewed and watched the woman, noticing that her pale green uniform buttoned up the back and was stretched open at the center, revealing her pink slip and under it a glimpse of the massive elastic strap of her brassiere.

The row of steaming coffee urns made Joey think about the times his father had taken him to the Ole's chili factory, where the chili was cooked in huge vats and served from similar urns in cream-colored ceramic bowls. You could smell the chili blocks away, even inside his father's Packard, the little fan mounted on the dashboard blowing the fog off the windshield, and Joey's mouth was watering by the time they went inside. The chili was hot and his father had shown him how to put in handfuls of the crisp oyster crackers that stood in large cream-colored bowls on the counter. Father said Ole's chili was the best anywhere, better at the factory even than in the cans at the market, and worth the special trip. Good as the chili was, for Joey the special thing was going somewhere with his father, just the two of them, doing a grown-up thing like eating chili together.

The woman was adding the cream and sugar to the bottles. She glanced at Joey and asked, What's your name?

Joey, ma'am.

Well, I'm Evelyn, Joey.

Glad to meet you, ma'am.

Call me Evelyn.

Sure, Evelyn, Joey answered, but it didn't feel right.

How is school going, are you learning a lot?

Joey swallowed the last of the jelly doughnut and said, Yes, ma'am, we're learning about other countries and it's real interesting.

You're a good boy, you got industry, you'll go far, not like some, she said, and glanced at the man at the end of the counter.

Well hell, the man muttered, the coffee run was my idea, wasn't it? The kid should pay me a commission.

Evelyn snorted and handed Joey the rack with the bottles filled, collected the money, and said, You be good now, and keep warm.

Joey said, Thank you for the doughnut, ma'am. He pulled up his muffler and went out into the cold street.

With the bottles full, the rack was heavy, but Joey was big for a ten-year-old and didn't have much trouble getting it back to the window, where the grateful men reached out their black hands with the white creased palms and took their bottles and disappeared into the steamy darkness of the factory. The boy was last and reached out a bony arm and took his chocolate milk. He lingered at the window, staring out at Joey, and Joey stared back through the rusty bars. One of the men called from inside, Hey, Booker T, you got to finish this floor 'fore the bossman gets back.

Not looking away from Joey, Booker T answered defiantly, Shit, I just gonna have my milk. He lifted the bottle to his lips. Joey watched the big Adam's apple on his neck bob up and down, his ears standing out from his head, his hair so short on his head he looked almost bald. It was as if knowing Booker T's name made Joey see him more clearly. Booker T finished his milk and looked out at Joey, his eyes huge.

Joey said, How you doin'?

Booker T said, Shit, how you think? and disappeared inside.

The first man reappeared and asked Joey if he could come by again after school, they could use an afternoon coffee break too, We gets sleepy after lunch, you know.

Joey was excited. Sure, just wash the bottles out and have them ready when I come back.

Joey hurried back home, avoiding the shortcut and going the long way around the block in the opposite direction so as to avoid being seen. As he rounded the corner, he had to step aside for the wagon pulled by the sway-backed horse with bells on its halter, driven by the old black man with a curly white beard who looked just like Uncle Remus in the Disney movie and whom the kids knew as the Regsaliar, because that was what he seemed to be singing as he went slowly up and down the alleys collecting junk, calling *Regs-a-liar*, though Joey's mother said he was actually saying Rags and Iron. Joey waved, and the old man nodded gravely to him and went on singing.

Joey ran the rest of the way home and down the stairs into the gangway. He made sure the coast was clear, put the rack back in its hiding place, retrieved his lunch, and went back out to the street. As he walked, he felt lighter, bigger. Some-thing had changed, changed profoundly.

The sun was reaching into the street now, it was a bit warmer, and Joey's breath no longer steamed. The horse-drawn produce wagon was already starting its daily trip down Twenty-Second Place, beautiful boxes of melons, lettuces, zucchini and multicolored squash, celery and all manner of fruit and vegetables displayed on tilted racks on both sides, the driver ringing his bell and calling *frutta e vegetali, frutta e vegetali*. Several women came down their steps, pulling their sweaters closed, carrying string bags to buy fresh produce for the day. Around the corner at the other end of the street, the man who sharpened knives and scissors came calling, *coltelli e forbici, coltelli e forbici*, pushing his handcart with the huge round sharpening stone that he turned by stepping on a board that hung below it. As he pushed his cart down the street, a peg on one of the wheels struck a gong that made a dissonant, haunting ding-dong.

At the end of the street, Joey stopped for a moment and listened to the ringing of the bells, the vendors' calls, the rapid, liquid Italian of the women, the clopping of the horse's hooves, the distant song of the Regsaliar. It was the music of his neighborhood, made sweeter by the shiny new dime he could feel in his pocket, the first money he had ever earned, truly and completely his, and he wanted to remember this moment as long as he lived.

4 THE BROTHERHOOD ASSEMBLY

MRS. SCHLAGLE WAS NOT THE ONLY STERN TEACHER at Pickard School. Miss McLaughlin, who taught Joey's afternoon class, was even meaner. When the class got noisy, she would pull out the bottom side drawer of her desk and pound on it with the end of her long wooden pointer. When she got really angry she yelled and her face got red and blue veins stood out on her neck, which Joey thought was a shame because most of the time she was a good-looking woman.

Miss McLaughlin was in charge of the three school assemblies staged each year by the sixth grade in the gymnasium, which was also the auditorium and had a raised stage at one end with curtains and lights. When they set up for an assembly, Joey, Peter, Walter, and the other boys would pull out the folding bleachers from the sides of the gym, pull the heavy drapes over the windows, and open the footlights that rotated out of the floor at the front of the stage. Since Joey was one of the larger boys in the class, Miss McLaughlin put him in charge of opening and closing the big red front curtain and raising and lowering the handles of the rheostats that controlled the stage lighting. Joey was fascinated by the long strips of colored lights that hung in rows over the stage and the spotlights mounted on pipes with their bulging lenses and colored filters, and the way the lighting changed when he moved the handles of the rheostats.

For the fall assembly last November, Joey's class had recreated the first Thanksgiving dinner, some of them dressed as pilgrims and some as Indians. Benita was Pocahontas, whose teepee stood by the shores of Gitchee Goomee, and she looked beautiful in the colored light as Joey stood backstage holding the rope that would raise the harvest moon. He was jealous when Walter Siroka, as Captain John Smith, put his arm around her. The second assembly of the year had been at Christmas, and Benita was again radiant as the Virgin Mary, and Joey was deeply disappointed when Miss McLaughlin picked Big Paulie to be Joseph. Now, on this day in early February, it was time to begin preparing for the third, springtime assembly.

The class was voluntarily quiet as Miss McLaughlin announced that they would stage a Brotherhood Week program, and that each of them would appear as a student from a different foreign country and give a speech about life in their homeland. Joey fully expected to be condemned to run the curtain and lights again, but was surprised when Miss McLaughlin said that he and Benita would be the Turkish boy and girl. When the scripts were passed out, Joey was overjoyed. The two of them shared a scene that was a whole page long.

After school that day, Benita caught up to him at the corner as he waited to cross Cermak.

We better practice, she said, we have a lot to say. You better come over to my house so we can work on it together.

Joey couldn't speak for a moment. To be invited to the Fantozzi house! It had never happened before to Joey or anyone he knew. Even Big Paulie, walking nearby, stole a sidelong glance at Joey with something like envy. Sure, Joey finally said, I'll just tell my Nonna and I'll be right over. Then he remembered his coffee run. He had promised the men in the factory to come right after school. What to do? Thinking fast, he said to Benita, I might be a little late, sometimes my Nonna needs me to go to the store for her or something.

Sure, come when you can. We don't eat until seven.

Joey left her at the corner of Oakley Avenue and watched her go up into the yellow brick house. At the door, she turned and waved. Joey waved back. When she was inside, he ran down Twenty-Second Place as fast as he could, dashed down the stairs and through the gangway to the back porch. Praying that his grandmother wouldn't see him, he got his wire basket from the cupboard, dashed through the alley, through the muddy snow in the empty lot, past the place of the kittens' execution, crossed Cermak in the middle of the block, dodging cars, ran to the factory window, almost slipping on the oily puddles, and called through the open window, Coffee! Coffee!

It was Booker T who came to the window holding a broom. Hi, Booker T, Joey said.

Booker T's eyes widened. How you know my name?

I heard them call you that this morning.

So what's your name?

I'm Joey, Joey said, and stuck his hand through the bar. Booker T looked at it but didn't know what to do. Awkwardly, Joey pulled it back. I'm in kind of a hurry, Joey said, Are the bottles ready?

Booker T said, All washed. He turned and started handing empty milk bottles out through the bars and Joey put them in the wire rack, which would not fit through the bars.

You want the same as this morning? Joey asked.

Yeah, sure, Booker T said, here's the money. As he passed out the coins, Booker T asked, What's the big hurry?

Joey tried to look modest and said, I got a kind of date.

Booker T raised his eyebrows. With a girl?

Yeah, Joey said, trying to sound nonchalant, what else?

Well, shit, Booker T said, ain't that something.

Joey hurried to the coffee shop. The big woman with the frizzy hair was still behind the counter. So, she said, this is a full-time job you got yourself.

Yes, Ma'am.

Well, a workingman needs his sustenance, she said, and again pushed the plate of doughnuts toward him while she filled the bottles. Joey gulped down a doughnut, this time with strawberry filling.

He paid and rushed out. I got to go, thanks again, see you tomorrow morning.

Sure thing, I'll be here.

Where else would you be, snorted the large man at the end of the counter.

Joey tried to run, but the full bottles clanked so hard against the wire rack that he was afraid they would break. As Booker T took his chocolate milk, he said, You have a good time with that girl now, hear?

Joey felt himself redden, and as he hurried away he turned back and called, Her name's Benita. Benita.

Joey could hear Booker T repeating the name, rolling it around in his mouth like candy. Bay-nee-tah!

Joey ran home, hid his wire rack, and ran upstairs where he found his grandmother cooking, as usual. Again trying to sound nonchalant, he said, *io sto andando su alla casa di Benita a praticare la nostra parte nel dramma*. I'm going over to Benita's house to practice our part in a play.

His grandmother looked up in alarm. *La casa di Benita? Lei va a lavare la Sua faccia e mani e pettina i Suoi capelli!* Benita's house? You go wash your face and hands and comb your hair! Joey started downstairs and his grandmother yelled after him, *E porsi calze pulite!* And put on clean socks!

Joey had to laugh. Socks! Nonna usually insisted on clean underwear, in case you were in an accident. But socks! Why would he need clean socks?

SCRUBBED AND COMBED, HE HURRIED DOWN THE STREET to the corner, pushed through the low, ornate iron fence, went up the steps to the front porch, and rang the bell. As he waited, he ran his finger along the smooth yellow pressed brick as one might caress the stone of a castle, and indeed, the Fantozzi house had always seemed to Joey like the lord's castle around which the peasant village of the neighborhood was clustered. Soon Mr. Fantozzi himself opened the door. He was a short, stout man with baggy pants, a red cardigan sweater, and a small, unlit black cigar in one corner of his mouth. He took out the cigar and said, Hello, you must be Dino's son, you look just like him, how's your mother, give them my regards. Augusta and Beppino too. Come on in.

Joey carefully wiped his feet on the jute mat that said *Benvenuto*, and followed the great man into the living room. The hallway was dark and hushed, it had a plush carpet that squished under Joey's feet; and velvet curtains at the living room door. Fan was saying, I've known your folks since they came over from the old country. Fine people. Fine family. There and here. Your dad and I had some good times when we were kids in Italy.

They entered the living room. Mrs. Fantozzi was sitting in an overstuffed chair, knitting. She was huge, and her sweater was stretched open between the buttons. Her gray hair was tied back in a tight bun, and she had on a hairnet that stretched over her head, tied in a knot on her forehead. Fan said, *Questo è Joey, il figlio di Dino. Lui è venuto a studiare con Benita.* This is Joey, Dino's son. He's come to study with Benita.

Mrs. Fantozzi smiled and lowered her knitting, saying, *Che giovane eccellente. Prenda via le Sue scarpe.* What a fine young man. Take off your shoes.

Joey was confused for a moment, then looked down at the white carpet under his feet. He sat on the sofa and slipped off his shoes, understanding now his grandmother's sage advice and wishing that he had followed it. He was relieved to see that there were no holes in his socks.

Wait right here, Fan said, I'll let Benita know you're here. He left and Mrs. Fantozzi returned to her knitting. Joey sat carefully on the clear plastic slipcovers and looked at the ornate furniture, so much more elegant than the maroon mohair sofa and chair in his own living room. There was no sound except the ticking of a baroque clock under a glass dome on the mantelpiece, and the rapid clicking of Mrs. Fantozzi's knitting needles. Above the sofa was a picture made of something like seashells and slivers of opalescent glass. Eager to break the silence, Joey asked, What is that a picture of?

Mrs. Fantozzi looked at him quizzically and said, *Non capesco.*

Remembering that she spoke no English, Joey asked, *Cosa è quell'un ritratto li?* Mrs. Fantozzi nodded and said. *Ah, sì, è Piazza di San Marco a Venezia.* There was another long silence as the needles clacked at a furious rate. Joey shifted and the plastic rustled under him. Sweat was beginning to form where his back touched the plastic. After a time, Mrs. Fantozzi said, *Come è il Suo Nonna Augusta*? How is your Nonna Augusta?

Joey answered, *Lei sta bene*. She's fine. Mrs. Fantozzi nodded, apparently satisfied that their conversational duty had been done. She said nothing more for the remainder of his visit.

Peter came into the room and said, Hi, Joey. So you gonna practice with Benita? Joey nodded. Peter turned to his mother and said, *Sto andando fuori a giocare*. I'm going out to play. There was no break in her rhythm as she nodded, and Peter was gone.

Finally Benita came in, looking freshly scrubbed and radiant, carrying a tray with some milk and *biscotti*. Hi, Joey, she said, sorry you had to wait. Joey answered, I'm sorry I was so long, I had to do some things.

Sure, that's fine, Benita said. They sat and nibbled *biscotti* and sipped milk for a while. The knitting needles clacked. Joey looked over at Mrs. Fantozzi, then at Benita. Benita gave a little shrug that made Joey understand that her mother would be keeping them company for the duration. Fortunately, Mrs. Fantozzi's presence didn't bother Joey one bit. Being an only child raised mostly by his grandmother, he was actually more comfortable with adults than with other children. In fact, he was relieved that he wouldn't suffer the awkwardness of being completely alone with Benita.

He took out the piece of paper with their speech on it, unfolded it, and said, I guess we better start.

When they had memorized their speech, they called Fan back in and recited it. Fan did a running translation for his wife and when it was over both of them applauded. Fan waved his cigar and said, You were just like real Turks. Joey and Benita shone with pride, and at the door Benita squeezed Joey's hand. Joey ran all the way home, barely touching the pavement.

That evening after dinner, Joey performed both parts of the speech for his folks, reciting Benita's lines in a high voice. Mother and Father applauded and were tremendously excited about his impending stage debut. Over the next few days, mother set to work making a Turkish costume by embroidering one of Father's old vests, and Father borrowed a fez from a Shriner he knew, even though good Catholics were not supposed to consort with Shriners. Father fitted the fez to Joey's head with newspaper folded inside the headband while telling him about the Italian folk plays the whole neighborhood staged during the Depression at the McCormick Works Clubhouse, and how it was in one of these plays that he and Mother had first noticed each other. Father had enjoyed performing when he was a young man, and he and some of his friends sometimes went downtown to the Lyric Opera and earned spending money as spear-carriers in productions of *Aida* and *Carmen*, and how thrilling it was to stand behind Tito Gobbi when he played *Rigoletto*, or Lily Pons as she sang about burning the candle at both ends in *Lucia*. The whole family loved opera and Nonna Severina could sing whole arias from *La Forza Del Destino* and Nonna Augusta especially loved *Rigoletto*. In fact, Nonna Augusta had given Father the middle name Rigoletto, which Joey thought was wonderful. As Joey thought about his part in the Brotherhood Day assembly, he began to feel that it was a call to his destined vocation; after all, he had the theatre in his blood!

The night before the assembly, Joey barely slept. He got up early and hurried to deliver the coffee to the factory. The woman at the coffee shop noticed that he seemed nervous, and he told her about the show, and she said, *Merde*.

What's that? Joey asked, and she laughed and said it meant shit in French, and that when she had been a dancer in New York they always said that instead of good luck, which was considered bad luck.

The man at the end of the counter snorted and said, You weren't no dancer in New York.

The woman swatted him with her dishtowel and said, Lot you know, I was some looker when I was young.

Maybe a stripper, then, the man said, and laughed until he started to cough up phlegm.

When Joey delivered the coffee, he said to Booker T, I'm going to be in a play today at school.

Booker T stared at him as if he were from another planet and said, You gonna get up in front of people and talk?

Joey tried to look as if this was the most normal thing in the world, and said, Sure.

Booker T shook his head and said, No way you get me to do that, I be scared to death.

Joey said, Hell, do it all the time. But his stomach was full of butterflies at the thought.

The assembly was to be in the last period, at two o'clock, and Joey's father was going to delay leaving for work and his mother was getting off early, so they could both be there. But first there was a dress rehearsal right after lunch and Joey was so excited he was afraid he might pee in his pants again. When it was their turn, he and Benita joined hands and came out onto the stage and stared into the darkness of the gymnasium, not able to see anything past the red, white and blue footlights. They did their speeches perfectly, and Miss McLaughlin didn't even have to yell, Louder! as she had for most of the other kids. When they were done, they went behind the curtains and Benita leaned over and kissed him on the cheek. Lenora Gonzini saw this and told the other girls, who giggled. Joey smiled at them defiantly.

As the dress rehearsal was nearing its end and Joey was waiting to close the big red curtain, Walter Siroka and Big Paulie started fighting backstage. Joey grabbed Walter to try to stop the fight and missed his cue to close the curtain. Miss McLaughlin ran up onto the stage yelling, What's going on, who is making all that noise? She saw the three of them, Walter and Paulie and Joey. All right, she yelled, pointing at the three boys, Go to the principal's office right now, you're all out of the program!

And so at two o'clock, when Joey's mother and father came to see the Brotherhood Day assembly, they had a conference with the principal instead and Benita had to be a little Turkish girl all by herself. As he sat in the principal's office dressed in his vest, holding the fez on his lap, watching the disappointment on his parents' faces, Joey swore to himself that someday he would become a famous actor and would come back and crush Miss McLaughlin.

The very next week justice was done. The high ceilings in Pickard School were covered with decorations of plaster scrollwork, and when Miss McLaughlin got mad about something and pounded her pointer into her desk drawer especially hard, a big chunk of plaster fell from the ceiling and broke on her head. After a moment of stunned silence, the class cheered like mad, Joey loudest of all, and Miss McLaughlin got red in the face and ran from the room and after a while another teacher came to take over and said that Miss McLaughlin was ill and wouldn't be back that day. In fact, she didn't come back the rest of that week. For Joey, it was the first proof of the existence of God, and the kids who were lucky enough to witness the miracle would remember it for the rest of their lives.

5 THE FURNACE ROOM AND OTHER MYSTERIES

THE SUNKEN FURNACE ROOM NEXT TO JOEY'S BEDROOM was a place of profound mystery. It was always locked, though Joey assumed it was not so much to keep him out as to keep unimaginable horrors in. He had only glimpsed the inside a few times while his father was working there, as he was today. Joey leaned through the door and asked, What'ya doin', Dad?

His father was kneeling beside a round object in front of the big red furnace that sat in the center of the room. Without looking up he said, I'm cleaning the blower.

Can I come in?

Sure, just be careful and don't touch anything.

Joey stepped down the three steps to the concrete floor. The room smelled of fuel oil, and the brick walls were coated with the fuzzy white accretion of dampness and age. Joey circled the furnace warily. Having originally been made to burn coal, it had a slatted iron door through which could be seen the blue flame of the fuel oil to which it had been converted by his father. A big iron pipe led through the room's outer wall to the large black metal oil tank in the back yard that was filled once a month from the Bell Oil truck that stopped in the alley, through a hose that was pulled in by a jolly man in blue overalls.

Above the red furnace was a large, round, galvanized metal cylinder studded with rivets, out of which ran several pipes. Out of its front stuck a large ominous pressure gauge. Joey stared up at it, enthralled. Father said, That's the pressure tank. It holds the steam from the furnace. The steam goes through those pipes to the radiators, and when the heat is out of it, it condenses back into water and comes back to be made into steam again.

Joey nodded, understanding. The radiators in each room fascinated him. Just last month he had watched his father paint them with a miraculous silver paint that Father said was made from banana oil. Joey had been allowed to do some of the painting, and had admired the radiators' simple gleaming shape. But he also felt a lingering fear of them as objects of power and pain. When he was six, his mother was making the beds and had piled pillows against one of the radiators. Joey jumped into them headfirst and hit the radiator by mistake and opened a gash on his forehead. At the hospital they gave him stitches without an anesthetic and it took his mother and three nurses to hold him down. He still had a small scar on his forehead. When he turned ten, Father had made it one of his chores to open the little valves on the bottoms of the radiators once a month, and collect in a mason jar the water that had condensed inside. He loved the little chrome canisters with pointy tops on the sides of the radiators that sometimes emitted plumes of steam. Father said they were safety valves, and Joey was intrigued by the idea that these heavy blocks of hot metal might someday explode. He sometimes touched them with his fingers to see how long he could stand the pain.

And here, in the red furnace and bulging pressure tank, was the source of all that power.

Joey noticed that most of the steam pipes ran up into the ceiling, but one of them ran from the tank, down the walls, and into a little tunnel at the floor. He knelt and peered into the darkness of the tunnel. His father told him that when they had moved into the basement years ago, it was not heated and the steam pipes ran only upstairs. So Father had dug this tunnel under the house to install new radiator pipes for the lower floor. Lying on his back, he had hacked it out and passed the dirt to Joey's mother in a bucket on a rope, like prisoners trying to escape, which, in a way, they were. Wow, Joey said, that was a lot of work.

Father looked up from his work on the blower and said, That wasn't the half of it. When you were a year old, right after we moved in, you came down with double pneumonia, and the doctor blamed it on the hot chimney pipe that used to run from the furnace through your bedroom to the outside wall. So I took it out and built a whole new chimney of bricks up the side of the house. It was hard, Father said, but it kept them warm, and the low rent charged by his parents was all they could afford in those days.

Father spoke of all this with pride, and Joey marveled at it. Father pointed over at the drain in the floor and told Joey to take a look. Across the drain was bolted a heavy steel plate with slits cut in it. You know why that's there? Father asked. Joey shook his head. When you were a little baby, Father said, we heard you screaming one night and we ran in and found a huge sewer rat, a foot long not counting the tail, in the crib with you. I hit at it and it ran back in here and went back down into that sewer. It had been strong enough to push the grate out of the drain hole. So I sat up for three nights in here with my shotgun, and when it came up again, I blew its head off. Then I made that new drain cover and bolted it to the floor.

Dino! Mother was at the door, having heard this recitation from the kitchen. What are you telling him? He's going to have nightmares.

Joey looked up and said, That's okay, ma, I'll be fine, nothing could get out of there now.

But in truth, Father's precautions were not altogether comforting to Joey, who could imagine slender and slimy things that might slither up through the slits in the grate from the fetid dark of the sewer below. Every night after that, while he waited to fall asleep, Joey listened to the furnace just on the other side of his bedroom wall making its low rumble and whir, purring like a huge red animal with glowing eyes that squatted beneath the maze of pipes and gauges, feeding on dark memories, ready to rise up and devour them all.

Though he tried not to think about it, over the following weeks Joey's fear of the furnace and the dark realm over which it presided grew. Soon he was having trouble falling asleep. He decided to confess his fears to his closest friend, Bruno Gini. Bruno was an older boy of sixteen, who lived across the street. His family had come from the same village in Italy as Joey's folks, and he was Joey's godfather, mentor, and confidant. They often played games together, Joey's favorite being Photoelectric Football. That next Saturday when they were playing at Bruno's house, Joey told him about the furnace room and his fears.

Bruno laughed, and said, Ours is even better, come on, I'll show you. They went down the back stairs, and Bruno opened the door to the Gini furnace room. The same smell of fuel oil greeted them. They stepped down into the room and Joey was surprised to see that the floor was dirt, not cement. And there was no red furnace and pressure tank; instead, in the center of the room stood a huge round black furnace with a Hydra's head of air ducts that ran up into the house above. When Joey asked about this, Bruno explained that their furnace produced hot air instead of steam. He led Joey around behind the furnace to a set of shelves against the back wall. He pulled aside the shelves and revealed, low on the wall, an old wooden door. Joey was trembling with excitement as Bruno pulled the door open. Behind it was the mouth of a tunnel that led in the direction of the back yard. Bruno took a flashlight from one of the shelves and crawled into the mouth. Come on, he said.

Joey hung back. Aren't there spiders or snakes or rats or something in there?

It's okay, I'll go first and make sure.

With anyone but Bruno, Joey would have been too afraid. It was like entering the realm beneath the sewer grate.

Come on, it's okay! Bruno called from inside the tunnel. Joey swallowed and crawled into the tunnel after him.

The floor was packed earth, and on it there were remnants of a track, like a small railroad. The walls and roof were spaced wooden planks that held back the dirt. They crawled for what seemed a long time. Ahead of him, Joey could see Bruno's form silhouetted by the flashlight beam, and behind him the dim patch of the doorway growing farther and farther away. Something like a spider's web brushed against Joey's face and he was suddenly seized by a terrible fear, worse than anything he had ever felt, and he was sure he was going to be buried alive. He couldn't breathe, couldn't move, couldn't even cry out. He just rolled up in a ball on the damp earth and whimpered.

Bruno swung the flashlight around and shone its beam on the tendrils coming between the boards in the roof and said, Those are just roots from a tree. Joey could see that this was true but still couldn't move. Finally, about ten feet ahead, light flooded the tunnel as Bruno pushed open a trapdoor. We're here, he said and shone the flashlight back at Joey. You okay?

Joey took a deep breath and said, Sure, fine, and got back on his hands and knees and scuttled toward the light as fast as he could. Bruno got out and helped Joey up. They were in the garage behind Bruno's house. Bruno opened the garage door and they looked out into the alley. Joey asked, What's this tunnel for?

Bruno shrugged, and said, I asked my father once, but he just said the damn thing had put my Nonno in jail and he wouldn't talk about it. My mother wants to fill it in, but my father says it's too much work.

THAT NIGHT AT DINNER Joey said he had seen the tunnel at Bruno's house. His mother said, You didn't go in there, did you? That thing is going to fall down someday and bury somebody, shame on Bruno for taking you in there.

But Joey said, No, Bruno just showed it to me, we didn't go inside.

Father said he knew all about the tunnel, had even been in it once.

Mother said, It was a long time ago and I don't want you ever going in there.

But why is it there? Why would anybody dig a tunnel under their back yard?

Father said, Have you ever heard of Prohibition? Joey shook his head. Well, said Father, It was a time when beer and wine and whiskey were illegal.

Don't be filling the boy's head with your stories, that was a wicked time.

Father smiled and went on. During Prohibition, the Gini house had a big still in it.

Still? Joey asked, and Father explained.

It was a thing that made booze. It had a boiler in the basement and the vat for the mash and the condensing coils reached right up through the floor into the second story. Bruno's grandfather Enzio put the bootleg whiskey it made into bottles and cases. Then he would run it out to his garage on a little cart that ran on the rails in that tunnel. Nobody could see it. Trucks from the Dearborn Laundry would pull into the garage from the alley. They had trapdoors in the floors, and the booze was brought up inside, and they would deliver it with the linens to the restaurants and speakeasies all over the West Side.

Joey was amazed. He thought, Wait till I tell Bruno. Then he remembered that Bruno had said the tunnel had sent his Nonno to jail, and he asked about that.

Father laughed. There was a big snowstorm one winter and the G-men went through the whole city to see which houses were hot enough to melt the snow off the roof quickly, and they knew those houses had stills inside because stills give off a lot of heat. So they raided the Gini house and caught Enzio in the tunnel with a cart full of hooch and tore down the still and put Enzio in jail, but Fan got him out after a few days. Everybody in the neighborhood was sorry when it happened because they all made a little extra money from the operation. Your own Nonno Beppino used to deliver the empty bottles to Enzio. And Gigi, the pharmacist at the Rexall, used to blend herbs and oils for flavoring, rubbing them in the palms of his hands. He added the flavoring to the raw alcohol to make scotch, or bourbon, or gin, or any kind of liquor you wanted. Gigi was a great guy, but one night he was driving in his Oldsmobile with Doc

Salvia the dentist, and when they stopped at the light on Western and Cermak, a car pulled up alongside and Doc Salvia ducked but Gigi didn't and got his head blown off by a shotgun. Some of us thought that maybe Doc Salvia, who was fooling around with the girlfriend of a Mafia captain, was the real target.

Dino! Joey's mother said sharply, That's not the kind of story to be telling a ten-year-old boy!

But his father's stories of the neighborhood's gangster past were Joey's favorites, and Joey begged him to go on, Tell the one about Bella Bruna again!

Mother shook her head. Honestly, you two, she said.

But there was no stopping Father. He told again Joey's favorite story about the day he was working as a waiter at Toscano's restaurant when Dago Dan, the union organizer, had a shootout across the street with Bella Bruna's husband, Piero. Dago Dan had been romancing Bella Bruna, a beautiful woman who ran the best restaurant on Oakley Avenue and was a bit of a flirt, and Piero had found out and sent word to Dago Dan that if he came around again he would blow his head off.

Dago Dan was not a man to take a challenge lying down, so one afternoon he pulled up in front of Bella Bruna's restaurant in his big yellow Stutz Bearcat touring car. He sat there for a few minutes to give the news of his arrival a chance to spread. The restaurant and the other stores on the street quickly emptied. The old men playing *bocce* in the lot next to the Po Piedmont Club came out into the street. Silvio the barber, with his rotating candy cane sign and glass case full of war souvenirs, came out, and so did his customers, one with the sheet still around his neck and lather on his face. When the crowd was big enough, Dago Dan got out of the Stutz. He was a short man, stocky, with a hairline mustache like Ronald Coleman's. He wore a brown striped Italian silk suit with a black shirt and broad floral tie and, like most of the neighborhood men, a wide-brimmed Borsolino hat tilted down over one side of his face.

Bella Bruna rushed out of the restaurant, her apron tied in a way that accentuated her ample bosom, and tearfully begged Dago Dan to leave, but Dan moved her aside with a manly gesture and drew with a flourish a huge pistol from under his coat. The crowd retreated into doorways and behind parked cars. Bella Bruna cried out and fell to her knees. Dago Dan marched slowly, resolutely, up the steps of the restaurant and disappeared inside. Everybody knew that Piero kept a shotgun behind the cash register and that a shootout was inevitable. There was absolute silence except for the tearful voice of Bella Bruna saying the Act of Contrition and asking God to spare the man she loved, though only God knew which man she meant.

After a long time, there was a tremendous volley of shots, sharp cracks from the pistol and deep booming roars from the shotgun. Then complete silence again. Even Bella Bruna held her breath. After a few minutes, Dago Dan came out, put away his gun and straightened his tie. Without so much as a glance at Bella Bruna, he got into the Stutz and drove away. Bella Bruna got up and, followed by the rest of the neighborhood, went gingerly inside. The place was pretty well shot up, the mirror behind the bar shattered and several tables overturned. At the back of the main dining room, they found Piero, sitting at a table smoking a Parodi cigar and sipping a glass of *Strega*. No one could figure out how the two men had managed to miss each other. Some of the old men thought that Piero and Dago Dan had cooked the whole thing up between them to teach Bella Bruna a lesson, and it must have worked because she mended her ways after that.

Joey's mother had been listening to this story while she washed the dishes, and now she said, Dino, shame on you, what a story to tell the boy, besides I wouldn't believe a word of it if my father hadn't been there himself. And you know, old man Baldi bled to death in Bruna's toilet when she cut him with a kitchen knife, accidentally of course, but that's a whole other story. Joey begged her tell it, but she just dried her hands on the dishtowel and said, Now Joey, you go to bed, that's enough for one night.

Father took Joey into the bedroom while Mother made the lunches for the next day. As he put on his pajamas, Joey asked, Whatever happened to Bella Bruna and her husband and Dago Dan?

Oh, Father said, Bella and Piero are still running the restaurant, but a few years after the shootout Dago Dan informed against the Mafia and was found dead in the trunk of his Stutz Bearcat with his genitals stuffed in his mouth.

That night as Joey fell asleep, he tried to imagine what it had been like in that amazing time called Prohibition, when the houses had stills inside that went right up to the roof and tunnels under the back yard and people got their genitals stuffed in their mouths and the neighborhood seemed so outrageously alive and his father and mother were young. And he didn't think about the red furnace or the horrors lurking beneath the drain even once before he fell asleep.

6 AFTER WORK

In April the weather finally broke, the air turned balmy, and spring came. The last of the snow washed into the sewers. The patch of ice on the next-door neighbors' sidewalk had been building up all winter, trampled into a thick glacier-like mass by passersby, but as the air warmed, it began to lose its grip on the cement. Every time he passed on his way to or from his coffee run at the factory, Joey kicked chunks of it into the gutter. On his way home this afternoon, he looked up at the neighbors' front window and the faded banner with its four stars, and thought about the four sons he only dimly remembered, loud, strapping boys. When he put his wire basket away in the cupboard under the back stairs, he took out the snow shovel and stiff-bristled snow broom and went back up onto the street. He dislodged the last chunks of ice, then set about sweeping the last of winter's detritus from the neighbors' pavement.

Joey was feeling good about this tiny and much belated contribution to the war effort when, for no apparent reason, he found himself thinking about Booker T. Joey had been faithful in his coffee runs for almost two months now, and the coffee woman had come to expect him every day just before eight and again right after school, and had his doughnut ready. It was always Booker T who met him at the window now, and they had begun to exchange brief pleasantries. Booker T always seemed eager for news of Joey's life, and Joey had begun to feel he was living for two, that his meager reports offered some compensation to Booker T for living like a caged animal in that hellish place. Joey decided he wanted to see Booker T without the bars between them.

It was almost five o'clock, still light in the lengthening spring days, when Joey finished cleaning the neighbors' sidewalk. He put away the broom and shovel and hurried across the alley and empty lot, up the now barren sledding hill, and stopped across the street from the factory. Autos, trucks, and streetcars rumbled by on Cermak Road as the evening rush hour got fully underway. After a few minutes, the electroplating plant whistle blew. Joey ducked behind a lamppost and watched as the factory doors opened and disgorged a stream of people. First came the white office workers, many stopping to light cigarettes, some loosening their ties and carrying their jackets, enjoying the warm spring air. Most headed for the parking lot at the far side of the building where they split into groups that shared rides from other parts of the city, or from the western suburbs. Their cars were nudging their way into the stream of traffic on Cermak Road when the black laborers, all of them men, began to come out. Some wore faded leather jackets and denim pants, some wore overalls, most carried black lunchboxes or paper bags. They moved to the corner and gathered in a tight knot on the safety island in the middle of the street between the streetcar tracks. Soon a streetcar stopped and as many as could squeeze aboard got on until the conductor rang the bell and waved the rest away. The streetcar pulled out, a solid mass of men, some standing on the running boards, and the queue on the safety island was replenished from those still waiting on the sidewalk.

The factory doors burst open again and a boisterous group of younger black men, laughing and gesturing wildly, came out. A few had changed into surprising after-work party clothes, striped suits with wide lapels and baggy pants with narrow cuffs, colored shirts and bright floral ties, and wide-brimmed fedoras. They strutted past the crowd waiting for the streetcar and moved into the parking lot where they got into two huge, shiny Cadillacs and pulled away, their car horns playing a jaunty little melody. Joey recalled that his father had once told him that groups of black workers shared what he called block cars, cars owned cooperatively by several men living on the same street. Joey thought that these musical Cadillacs must be block cars.

Finally the last workers emerged from the factory, a gaggle of black cleaning women in frayed coats, their hair tied up in bandanas, chatting energetically. With them were three quiet young boys, Booker T one of them. Booker T looked even smaller and younger than he had through the window. His pants and jacket were too large, his closely shaved head bare, his shoes loose on his feet so that he shuffled slightly as he walked, looking at the ground, not joining in the conversation that swirled around him.

As the group of cleaning women and boys moved toward the streetcar stop, Joey walked parallel to them on the other side of the street. At the corner, Booker T looked across and saw Joey. He gave no sign, but Joey knew he recognized him. Joey crossed the street and approached him. Booker T looked away, but Joey said, Hello, Booker T. How ya' doin'?

What you want? Booker T answered, without looking at Joey.

I just wanted to see how you were.

Without turning, Booker T said, So now you seed me. How'd you expect me to be? Joey didn't know what to say next.

One of the men waiting for the streetcar came across to them. Well, the man said, if it ain't the coffee boy. What brings you here outside of work time? Joey looked up and recognized the man who had first given him the coffee money. In the daylight, his blue-black skin shone and his teeth flashed when he smiled. He was not a big man, but powerfully built, his upper body strong from years of moving heavy metal parts in and out of the chemical vats. He had an easy grace that put Joey at ease.

Joey said, I just wanted to see how Booker T was, sir.

That word, sir, registered on the man's face and he drew himself up a little. Well, he said, why don't we get introduced proper? What's your name? We can't be calling you coffee boy all the time.

Joey stuck out his hand and said, My name is Joey, sir.

The man looked at Joey's hand for a moment with surprised amusement, then took it. They call me Luther, he said, I'm Booker T's uncle. He turned to Booker T and said, Say hello to Joey proper, Booker T.

Booker T, still looking away up the street, mumbled, I knows him well enough. Joey stuck out his hand toward Booker T, but there was no response.

Luther said, Now, Booker T, that ain't no way to be, shake the boy's hand. Booker T stuck his hand out in Joey's general direction. Joey took it. It was cold and damp and hard with calluses. They shook once.

Then Booker T said, I better get in line. He moved away toward the corner.

So, Joey, Luther said, you go to the school next door.

Yes, sir, Joey said. He pointed across Cermak toward the empty lot, and added, I live right over there, on Twenty-Second Place.

Luther looked and nodded. That's real convenient, you can walk right to school. Lucky for us, too, you can get us the coffee. There was an awkward silence for a moment, then Luther said, You got to forgive Booker T. Through the window's one thing, but out here, in the daylight… well, he don't like people to see him in his work clothes.

Joey said, I was wondering about him working.

You mean, why he ain't in school too?

Yes, sir.

Luther looked at Joey a moment and said, You got folks I guess?

Yes, sir, my dad works in a factory too, and my mom works at Samsonite.

Luther nodded, taking this in. You a lucky boy, two folks workin'.

Joey shrugged. I guess, but I don't see them much except on the weekends.

Yeah, well, Booker T ain't got that much. He don't see his folks never.

Joey looked over toward Booker T, and their eyes met. Joey could not make out the expression on Booker T's face. Suddenly Booker T bolted and ran across toward the safety island without looking. Luther darted forward and yelled, Booker T! A car was coming in the inside lane and it slammed on its brakes, almost hitting Booker T, who was just barely pulled out of harm's way by Luther.

The driver of the car, a fat white man, rolled down his window and yelled, You crazy picaninny, why don't you watch where you're goin'! Then he realized there was a crowd of black men and women on both sides of his car, staring in at him. He hurriedly rolled up his window and pulled away. The workers on the island watched him go impassively, then turned and pressed forward as a streetcar came to a stop.

Luther turned back to Joey and called, We got to get this one, Joey, see you tomorrow. He took Booker T by the arm and they sprinted across to the island, where they were swallowed up in the mass of men and women. They managed to get one of the last spots on the running board as the streetcar pulled away. Joey watched it go, swaying, the trolley on the overhead wire emitting a shower of sparks as it crossed the junction at Oakley Avenue. Luther looked back and raised one hand slightly. Joey raised his hand in response. He thought he caught a glimpse of Booker T looking back at him as the streetcar was swallowed up in traffic.

7 THE BLACKBIRD HUNT

All through the Depression years, on every Saturday during the spring nesting season, the men of the neighborhood went out together to hunt in the farmlands to the northwest of the city, just as men had done for generations in the old country. They occasionally got pheasant or rabbit, but the most plentiful and reliable game was blackbirds, which they brought back by the hundreds. Now that the Depression had passed and times were better, the blackbird hunt continued, though only once each spring. It had become a purely social event, an occasion for camaraderie and affirmation of a common heritage for the men of the neighborhood. Most importantly, it served as an initiation ritual for the boys who were passing into adolescence. And so, in this spring of his tenth year, Joey's dad took him on his first hunt.

At four A.M. Saturday morning, the sky still dark, a long caravan of cars filled with men and boys formed on Oakley Avenue, coming from as far away as Twenty-Eighth Street. It seemed to Joey that every male in the neighborhood was there, even some he had before only glimpsed at church or at festivals. Father drove the Packard near the front of the line. In the passenger seat was Matseo, the carpenter with no left thumb, and in the back sat Joey and Bruno, a basket full of provisions between them. Bruno's dad had died some years before, and he had been more or less taken into Joey's family for occasions such as this. Bruno had been on his first hunt some five years before, and he understood the importance of the event for Joey. He leaned close to Joey and whispered, Just watch me and do what I do, just like in church.

In the car at the head of the line Joey could see Peter, also an initiate, riding in the back of Mr. Fantozzi's big Oldsmobile. Fan stood beside the car like a general at the head of his troops, lit his small black cigar, the flame briefly illuminating his face, then gave a signal with a flashlight. Car engines throbbed to life all up and down the line and those who were not yet aboard rushed to get in. Headlights were turned on. As they pulled out, Joey and Bruno waved like crazy at Mother, Nonna, and Alba, Bruno's mother, and even Mrs. Fantozzi and Benita, who stood in the crowd of women and girls under the streetlight at the corner, seeing their men off like troops going into battle. Joey's eyes sought out Benita's, and it seemed to him she was smiling at him with a special warmth that dispelled the chill of the night. Their gaze held until the cars turned onto Cermak Road and headed west.

The caravan wound its way north and west for an hour, the sky growing light behind them over Lake Michigan. The last vestiges of the city and suburbs melted away and they passed into the farmlands beyond, through the rural town of Naperville, and finally off the paved highway onto gravel roads. They passed between silent fields of corn and alfalfa glistening with dew, and pulled up at a field adjoining one of the sloughs in which the blackbirds roosted. There they parked the cars out of sight behind a line of trees. Father said that this field, rented for a small sum from a friendly farmer, had been the site of the hunt for years.

Everyone piled out of the cars and took turns holding the barbed wire fence up for others to crawl under. Guns in their cases and picnic baskets were passed through. A hearty breakfast was the first order of business, and blankets were spread and hampers opened. The grass was still wet, but everyone sat happily on the ground. Slices of unsalted Tuscan bread swabbed with jellies and marmalades, *biscotti*, and even containers of scrambled eggs and pancetta were consumed, along with thermoses full of coffee.

After the meal, the preparations for the hunt began in earnest. Guns were taken from their cases and cleaned and oiled, hunting vests were donned and stocked with shells. Father had brought for Joey the only spare gun in the family, Nonno's ancient ten-gauge Browning shotgun. It hadn't been used in years, but it had been oiled and stored in soft cloths and shone a deep blue-black. Joey was fascinated by the ornate scrollwork on its barrel and stock, and Father explained to him the intricacies of a Damascus barrel, formed from a coil of steel ribbon. Father showed Joey how to hold the huge gun, but it was so heavy Joey could barely keep it pointed skyward. The first time Joey fired it as a test, the recoil threw him on the ground, and everyone laughed. Old man Fantozzi stepped forward and helped Joey up, saying, That shoulder's going to be black and blue for a week. Hey, Peter, get Joey that extra gun, it's in the car. Peter trotted over and retrieved a smaller .410 shotgun, handed it to Joey and clapped him fraternally on the back. Thus anointed by the Fantozzis, a beaming Joey took his place in the line of hunters that stretched across the field, parallel to the edge of the slough that lay beyond.

As the sun broke behind them, the blackbird flock began to leave its roost. For many minutes, the sky was dark with thousands of birds as they passed overhead, so thick that the hunters fired almost without aiming, reloading as quickly as possible when their smoking guns were empty. Joey's dad showed him how to fire at an angle that would make the falling birds land in a pile right at his feet. The skill of each hunter could be judged by the size of his pile of birds, and the men competed good-naturedly, and hooped and hollered as the firing continued.

When the last of the birds had left the roost and the shooting was over, some of the wounded birds were still alive and fluttered in the pile, and Father showed Joey how to take these birds by the head and flip the body quickly, breaking the neck. The men then loaded the birds into sacks and bushels and old pillowcases, and put them into the cars and trucks. In the midst of the laughter and mutual congratulations, Joey was numb with shock. This carnage was not at all what he had expected.

By the time the birds had been collected and loaded, the sun was well up and warm. Joey was horrified to learn that they had to spend the entire day in the field until the flock returned to its roost in the late afternoon. They sat lazily in the grass in little groups, the older men smoking and playing cards, and all the boys together to one side. Big Paulie and even Rex and his gang were along, and by some unspoken agreement, a truce suspended all hostilities and rivalries among the boys. Even Rex seemed benign and once even smiled at Joey, as if they now shared some secret known only to young Tuscan males. Thus they spent the morning, the older boys telling stories of past hunts and generally being manly.

Soon it was time for lunch, and again the hampers were opened. Huge *panini* were assembled of *prosciutto, mortadella, coppicolo*, and *provolone*, with jugs of wine for the men and jars of the juice called *Tamarindo* for the boys. Joey tried to make a show of eating, but he could barely swallow and felt sick to his stomach. When anyone looked at him, he tried to hide his horror, but his eyes were glazed as he wrestled with the images of the dying birds and the gleeful blood lust of the men. He had to get away, at least for a moment, and went into the cornfield that adjoined the killing field on the pretext of peeing. The corn was just barely head high. Joey began to run through the rows, deeper and deeper. Bruno saw him go and followed.

Hey, Joey! Bruno called as they flashed through the rows of corn. When Joey heard Bruno's voice, he stopped, panting. Pretty tough, isn't it? Bruno said when he caught up.

Yeah, Joey answered, I pretty much hate it.

Bruno gave Joey a sympathetic glance and reassuring squeeze of the arm. Listen, Joey, you can get through this. It's only once a year, they used to do this a lot more often. At least we're going to eat them, it's not just killing. Okay?

Joey said, Okay, and they went back to the group.

After lunch, the afternoon was filled with games of marksmanship and hide and seek in the cornfield and more hours of storytelling. As the sun lowered in the sky, the line of hunters formed again, and as the flock returned to the slough, the whole grisly ritual repeated itself. With all the skill he could muster, Joey tried to avoid hitting any birds, but even so there was a small pile of dead and dying at his feet when the shooting stopped. Peter came by to collect his gun and commiserated with Joey over his poor showing, saying, That's okay, Joey, you'll do better next year. To himself, Joey promised that there would be no blackbird hunt, no hunt of any kind, for him next, or any, year.

When the caravan of hunters returned that evening, they were greeted as heroes by all the women and girls of the neighborhood. Benita ran forward to meet Joey as he climbed out of the car, asking, How did you do? Did you get a lot?

Yes, Joey said, a lot.

Good for you, Benita said, I knew you'd do good.

The women took the bags and bushels full of dead birds and distributed them equally to all the neighborhood households, whether they had participated in the hunt or not. That warm spring evening, everyone sat in clusters on their front steps, the women plucking the birds and gossiping, the men sipping *Campari* or *Strega* and smoking the dark little noxious Parodi cigars that everyone called Dago Ropes, recounting the heroic exploits of that day and other hunts of years past.

The next day, in every neighborhood house, Sunday dinner consisted of the cleaned blackbirds, the heads still on, cooked in meat sauce with black olives and wine, *a la cacciatore*, and served over great mounds of polenta, the yellow corn meal mush that to Joey tasted like shredded cardboard. It was one of the peasant dishes from the Old World that had been an economic necessity during the Depression and now was a tradition in the neighborhood. The tiny drumsticks were good for one pass through the teeth, like *hors d'oeuvres* on a toothpick, and the breasts were sucked off the carcass. The women reminded everyone to watch out for the buckshot, for there was surely a bit of lead in each bird, and this was no more feared in those days than was the lead in the paint that covered the walls of the children's rooms. Joey had gone to church that morning and had secretly prayed for forgiveness for his part in the hunt, and went back to bed complaining of a stomach ache, and so missed the feast. His mother told him not to worry, though, they would save him some.

In unguarded moments, Joey's mother allowed as how the labor of plucking and cooking the small birds was scarcely worth the meat they provided, and there was no complaint from the neighborhood women when years later blackbirds were placed under the protection of an international treaty, the hunt ended forever, and anonymous pieces of chicken replaced the blackbirds atop the Sunday polenta.

8 POKER IN THE KITCHEN

PICKARD SCHOOL HAD NO CAFETERIA so most kids brought a bag lunch and ate in their homeroom or, on good days, in the schoolyard. But those who lived nearby, and who had family at home during the day, had special permission to go home for lunch. Joey was one of these, and every day at lunchtime, except for the Monday piano lesson, he hurried across Cermak and the empty lot to eat with Nonna. She always had lunch ready for him, usually some warmed-up leftover spaghetti or boiled beef, and he would eat while she played the radio and went on with her endless cooking or baking, talking constantly to him in Italian.

Like most of the older people in the neighborhood, Nonna Augusta spoke almost no English. Nonno and Nonna had come to America during the great wave of immigration of the 1910's, bringing Joey's father with them, and had settled in this Chicago neighborhood with other people from the same cluster of Tuscan villages no more than twenty miles apart. Being among their own people, the elders had no need for English. As a result, the neighborhood was divided into three linguistic groups. Those over fifty spoke only Italian, and out of deference to them, conversations at home and at large family gatherings were mostly in Italian. The second generation, like Joey's mother and father, were fluently bi-lingual. Joey's folks even used Italian as a kind of secret code when they went shopping and wanted to discuss something without the salesperson understanding, though Joey found this acutely embarrassing. For the third generation, the neighborhood kids of Joey's age, Italian was barely a second language and they knew only enough to communicate with their elders, and that only at home. They would be the last generation to speak Italian at all. Joey, however, was an exception. Because his mother worked days and his father nights, Joey spent a lot of time with his grandmother, and as a result he spoke more Italian than English. In fact, that fall, Mrs. Schlagle had sent a note home saying that Joey was slow in his language development.

The note had caused an uproar. Joey's father remembered all too well how he had been taunted for his poor English when he started school in America, and he was terrified Joey wasn't growing up to be a good American and would suffer as he had. After much argument, Italian was outlawed in the home, at least in Joey's presence. This was hard on Nonno and Nonna, but they did what they could to incorporate a few English words into their vocabulary. The new-fangled refrigerator that had replaced the old *ice-a-boxey* was now the *refrigidere*, though the vacuum cleaner was still the *spiropolvio*, the dust breather. Whenever Joey was alone with his grandmother, however, as he was during lunch, her suppressed Italian poured out in a flood.

There were two radio programs that Nonna Augusta played during every lunch hour. The first was *Warehouse 49*, in which a pianist named Don Artiste went from piano to piano, playing a tune on each. The announcer crooned introductions, saying, Next, Don Artiste moves to a lovely blonde Baldwin spinet for his rendition of "The Sword Dance" from Rimsky-Korsakov's *Scheherazade*. Joey thought all the pianos sounded alike. After fifteen minutes and four or five pianos, *Warehouse 49* gave way to *The Hartz Mountain Canary Hour*, which, despite its name, was also only fifteen minutes long. It consisted entirely of a chorus of well-fed canaries singing *a capella*. Nonna had a canary of her own, named Lucia, in a cage by the kitchen window.

Lucia was the third or fourth bird that had inhabited the cage, her predecessors having either succumbed to drafts or made their escapes out the window while the newspaper in the bottom of the cage was being changed. After a minute or two of listening to the radio canaries, Lucia would join in and sing her little heart out, as did canaries in other kitchens all over the neighborhood. On summer days when all the kitchen windows were open and they could hear one another, they went on singing even after the radio program ended, and on summer afternoons the neighborhood was filled with their song.

On this spring day, Joey sat eating some leftover spaghetti re-cooked with olive oil and capers, listening to Lucia sing. Her song always made him remember how, during one of these lunch hour concerts three years ago when he was in the third grade, the radio canaries had suddenly fallen silent. There was only static for a time, and Nonna had given the old Philco a slap, as she sometimes had to do. But then, outside, the church bells started ringing at St. Michael's, and were joined by bells from churches in the surrounding neighborhoods. The factory whistle across the street blew, and distant whistles joined in from every direction. There was a buzz from the Philco and a quiet voice came on, sounding thin and tense. Joey had moved closer and stared at the loudspeaker in the big upright radio with the maroon grill cloth behind the gothic arches of its dark wooden case. The voice said slowly, President Franklin Delano Roosevelt died today in Warm Springs, Georgia.

Though she didn't understand, Nonna knew that something was wrong. *Accadde cosa?* she asked.

Joey managed to stammer, *Il presidente è morto.*

Oh Dio, Nonna gasped, crossed herself, sat down heavily, and began to sob. Joey comforted her as best he could, then went out onto the street. People were coming out of their houses, wandering around like they were lost. Some gathered in little knots on the front steps of the houses and held each other. The church bells continued to toll and the factory whistles to blow until the sun set.

Ever since that day, whenever they went to the movies at the Illington Theatre on Western Avenue, the projectionist started the show by putting up a slide of FDR in profile against a black background, and everyone in the theatre clapped and cheered. Joey never stopped marveling that so many people could love one person so much, or that a community could come together in shared grief and find strength and hope in one another like this. Years later, when he was grown, Joey would again hear the news of a fallen president, and the factory whistles would blow and the church bells toll and the people cry in the streets, and he would then remember how it had been when FDR died and take some comfort from it.

JOEY ALWAYS RUSHED HOME FROM HIS AFTER-SCHOOL COFFEE RUN on Thursdays in great anticipation. This was the one afternoon when Nonna Augusta suspended her cooking, and five of the older women from the neighborhood gathered in her kitchen for a furious game of poker. The women were greeted at the front door with great hilarity. It was a holiday for each of them. Alba Gini, Bruno's mother, was always the first to arrive, followed by Big Paulie's appropriately large mom, then Fosca Zanardo, the wife of the market owner. Always last to arrive was Mrs. Fantozzi, the doyen of neighborhood society. She was accorded special deference, lowering her great bulk into the chair normally reserved for Nonno Beppino at the head of the table. Each woman took from her copious purse a cigar box or coffee can full of folding money and coins and placed them in a pile on the table with ritual care. Two new decks of cards were unwrapped, one shuffled while the other was dealt, so there was almost no interruption between games. They had only an hour, and a lot of poker to play. Joey couldn't keep up with the blur of the women's hands as they made bets and split up pots, all the while filling the kitchen with a constant stream of gossip that flowed over and through the game.

Joey sat enthralled beside Nonna. She carefully lifted a corner of her cards to show him her hand. She was a serious player, and Joey quickly learned that he could make no sign of pleasure or displeasure at what he saw in her hand. Gradually, he began to understand the rules of the few games they played, nothing fancy, mostly five-card stud or draw. Joey was surprised that Nonna often won even when she didn't have the best hand. At these times she would throw down her cards without showing them to the others and if Joey made any sign of surprise or celebration, she would glare him into silence so fiercely it chilled his blood.

Joey had suspected Nonna's passion for gambling. He was an avid and secret explorer of closets and drawers, and one day had been poking around in Nonna's closet and found, behind the black leather shoes with the fat heels and the slits at the sides to accommodate her enormous bunions, a very heavy cigar box. When he opened it, he was amazed to find it full of silver dollars. He knew that in addition to her Thursday poker games, Nonna also went every Saturday to the horse races at the nearby track, which in those days paid winners in silver dollars. This treasure trove proved her skill as a handicapper. Each of these large, heavy coins represented a week's worth of coffee deliveries, and Joey was tempted to take a few, but he sensed that they had much more than monetary value for his grandmother, and besides, she was sure to have counted them. He closed the box and carefully put it back as he had found it. He never told anyone what he had found, for he understood that Nonna kept her substantial winnings secret from Nonno and the rest of the family. Her secret was safe with him, and he watched her play poker with even greater respect from then on.

Nonna's kitchen was in many ways the center of Joey's universe. Like all the older women of the neighborhood, she spent most of her time cooking, and Joey loved to sit in the kitchen while she worked, immersed in an ocean of wonderful odors. Like all the older people in the neighborhood, Nonna had grown up in Tuscany, and her cooking remained staunchly northern Italian. The family favorites for everyday meals were *Tortellini* or *Tagliatelle en brodo*, boiled beef, roast chicken with fresh sage and crusty potatoes, pasta in homemade meat sauce with meatballs or sweet sausage, and for dessert the crisp, flat, sweet *Briscitini* made in the two-handled press, or most often, almond-flavored *Biscotti* which were always in plentiful supply. He watched carefully as she made them.

BISCOTTI ALLA AUGUSTA
5 c sifted flour
5 t baking powder
6 eggs

½ lb (2 sticks) melted sweet butter
1 ½ c sugar
pinch of salt
2 T anise seeds, moistened
2 T anise flavoring
½ c sliced almonds

Sift the flour and baking powder together. Beat the eggs. Slowly add melted butter and sugar to the egg mixture, adding a pinch of salt. Blend this into the flour well. Add the anise seeds, flavoring, and almonds. Make a firm dough and knead until silky. Roll out in thin, long logs about 3 inches wide. Place these on a cookie sheet sprinkled with corn meal, and brush with melted butter. Bake in 350° oven about 15 or 20 minutes until lightly browned. Cut diagonally while still hot. Allow to cool and harden. If desired, toast lightly before serving.

The smells of his grandmother's cooking never left Joey. He sometimes thought that if he had to die, he would choose to die in the kitchen, his last breath infused with the smell of chicken roasting with fresh sage, or of almond-flavored *biscotti* baking.

9

AROUND THE PHILCO

After spending most afternoons soaking in the aromas of his grandmother's kitchen, Joey didn't look forward to his own family's dinner downstairs. Father had stopped working the afternoon shift and had switched to a normal schedule, and was now able to drive Mother to work in the morning on his way to Tractor Works and pick her up on the way home. They got home after dark, tired and hungry and eager to eat. Hurried and on a limited budget, Mother usually made dinner from cans and mixes. Joey was especially sick of Lipton's Noodle Soup, which came in small packets that, when mixed with water, produced a thin broth with tiny noodles, so salty it had to be watered down.

Dinnertime was made even less inviting by Father's endless complaints about his job. Like both his grandfathers, Joey's dad worked for International Harvester at Tractor Works on Western Avenue. He was the foreman of a machine shop, and it was a job he had come to hate. For one thing, he blamed it for giving him a chronically bad back. To make matters worse, one of his boyhood pals had become a vice-president of the company, and though a foreman's job seemed important to Joey, his father was ashamed that he had not risen further in the company. He blamed this on his lack of formal education, having been forced to leave grade school before graduation in order to go to work and support his family during the Depression. His frustration produced long diatribes against the current management of the company, men who had none of the common sense and unpretentious friendliness of the founders, who had themselves been unschooled and had worked shoulder-to-shoulder with their men in the early days.

Father's lack of formal education was made even more painful by Mother's acknowledged position as the smartest of her family. She had been valedictorian of her high school class, and had even been awarded a scholarship to the University of Chicago. She had been prevented from accepting it, however, when her father, Nonno Lorenzo, had decided that the family could afford only one child in college, and her older brother, Uncle Louis, had been sent to engineering school instead. As unfair as this seemed to Joey, it seemed to be accepted as a matter of custom by everyone in the family, including his mother who, though she told him the story with some sadness, explained that in the Old Country the eldest brother always came first, certainly before a mere girl, and so it was understandable that it should be the same in the New World. What bothered Joey more than the injustice, though, was that his mother seemed to go out of her way to avoid appearing smart for fear of inflaming his father's already strong sense of intellectual inadequacy.

Thankfully, the hours after dinner were as pleasant as dinner was unpleasant. This was Joey's favorite time of the day. On every weeknight, he got into his pajamas right after dinner and took his place in front of their big Philco radio, just like the one upstairs in Nonna's flat, and listened to his favorite shows. First was *The Green Hornet* with his faithful sidekick Cato, who started out Japanese, but had miraculously become Filipino after Pearl Harbor. Next was *Captain Midnight*, who ended every show with a secret message that Joey could decode using his secret decoder ring that had finally come in the mail after the necessary number of Wheaties box tops had been collected and sent in. During these kids' shows, Father and Mother cleaned up the dinner dishes, then joined him around the Philco, whose yellow dial glowed like a fire on the family hearth and gave off a tangible warmth. Together they listened to *The Shadow*, who knew what evil lurks in the hearts of men and whose real name was Lamont Cranston; *Gangbusters* with real cases from the files of the FBI; and later, depending on the night, one of the national favorites that in summer could be heard coming from the open windows of every house on the street, shows like *Amos 'N Andy, The Lux Radio Theater, The Life of Reilly* with William Bendix, and Joey's favorite, *Fibber McGee and Molly* with Fibber's wonderful closet that once in every show loudly spilled its contents.

The radio's dominion over the family, however, had come to an end that spring. Joey's father was always first in the neighborhood with gadgets like a movie camera and a wire recorder, so it was no surprise when he brought home the neighborhood's first television set, an enormous Capehart-Farnsworth console with a radio and pull-out record changer. It was carried down the cement stairs by four delivery men and brought into the house through the front door, which Joey had never before seen opened and which had to be pried and beaten before it yielded. The Capehart-Farnsworth, with its miniscule oval screen, loomed like a colossus in the living room, and the radio shows were replaced in Joey's life by a tribe of puppets, *Lucky Pup* with

Pinhead and Foodini, *Kukla, Fran and Ollie*, and *Howdy Doody* with Buffalo Bob, Clarabelle the Clown, Princess Summerfallwinterspring, and the Peanut Gallery. On Saturday mornings Joey now watched the televised *Big Top Circus* program with the beautiful, blond drum majorette Mary Hartline, for whom Joey felt his first pangs of something like lust, imagining her high stepping and twirling her baton in nothing but her white boots and shako.

In the evenings after dinner, the family now gathered to laugh uproariously at Milton Berle, or *Your Show of Shows* with Sid Caesar and Imogene Coca, or Steve Allen, or *The Ed Sullivan Show*, sometimes with Joey's favorite, the ventriloquist Señor Wences. On Saturday nights his parents let Joey stay up late to watch *The Ernie Kovacs Show*. Kovac's humor seemed to Joey a whole new way of looking at the world. He began to see the things in his life that made no sense as if they were sketches on the Kovacs show, and he was especially struck by the sketch of the three monkeys of the Nairobi Trio, with their mechanical repetitions that always ended with one hitting another on the head. This routine made Joey think of the men in the electroplating factory endlessly dunking racks of metal parts in the steaming vats, with Booker T as the smallest and saddest monkey who got hit on the head at the end.

As Joey thought about it more, the tribe of monkeys increased and came to include his own father at Tractor Works, and the jobs of countless others, jobs that seemed as mindless and hurtful as the comical machinations of the three monkeys. He made himself a promise that no matter what, he would never become a monkey and let his life become an Ernie Kovacs routine.

10 CHURCH

On Sunday mornings Joey would jump into his parents' bed and snuggle between them, and his mother would read the funny papers to him, panel by panel, just like the man on the radio, only better. When she was done, Joey had to get dressed and go to Mass at St. Michael the Archangel's, as their modest neighborhood church was grandly called, while his folks stayed in bed. Joey resented this and thought it was hypocritical of his folks to send him to church alone. His Nonna and Nonno didn't go to church either. In fact, Nonno Beppino, who was a life-long socialist and had read Gibbon, dismissed the church as an oppressive institution that ran unholy activities like Bingo. Once, when the parish priest had come to the house to try to persuade Beppino to come to church, the old man had sent him packing, saying he didn't frequent brothels.

Despite his grandfather's resistance and his parents' antipathy, Joey, like all the children in the neighborhood, was raised a proper Roman Catholic. The parish priest, Father Louis Donovan, had once proclaimed that if you gave him a boy until he was seven he would make him a Catholic for the rest of his life, and three years ago, right on schedule, seven-year-old Joey had received his First Holy Communion. Joey and Benita and their pals had been prepared for this milestone in their spiritual journey by a series of catechism classes conducted by Father Louis himself. He was a stern Irish priest, built like a fire hydrant with a brightly veined red nose. His foul temper was probably due to finding himself stuck in an all-Italian working-class parish, although he did little that might endear him to his flock. Indeed, Father Louis was widely unpopular, and his fall from grace began soon after his arrival when he had announced that henceforth St. Michael's would conduct silent collections, meaning that all donations were to be in paper money, no coins.

In catechism class Father Louis had explained the proper way to make the Sign of the Cross, and the significance of each of the stations. He had just finished discoursing on the Holy Ghost when he noticed that Paula Parmentoni, Joey's third cousin, was using her left hand to make the Sign. He descended on her, yelling that she was insulting God, how could she be so stupid as to not know her right from her left. Now, it happened that Paula's parents ran the neighborhood pasta factory, the pride of which was an automatic ravioli machine that cut, filled, and pressed the little squares of pasta. Paula helped out in the factory after school, and the first time she tried to run the ravioli machine she got her right arm stuck in it, and was left with a stump that extended just short of her elbow. So that day in catechism class, when Father Louis took a breath during his tirade about the right versus the left hand, Paula simply opened her coat and stuck out her stump. The look on Father Louis' face was to be forever one of Joey's most treasured memories, surpassed only slightly by that of the plaster hitting Miss McLaughlin on the head.

On the day before the actual Communion ceremony, Sister Mary Ignatius had distributed black armbands to the thirty or so kids receiving the sacrament. This armband, she said, was not only a sign of eternal mourning for the death of the Redeemer, but also signified the purity of the wearer. Therefore, it had to be burned the first time they committed a mortal sin, though venial sins were allowed as long as they were promptly confessed. After cataloging the differences between venial and mortal sins, she told with great feeling the story of an old man of the parish who, on his deathbed, had asked the priest to look in the drawer of his dresser. There the priest had found the old man's black arm band, still intact after seventy years of pious living, seventy years containing not a single mortal sin. This moral tale failed to impress Joey. Considering the differences between mortal and venial sins he had just learned, he was convinced that venial sins were hardly worth the effort. The old man, he thought, had wasted a lot of opportunities.

The First Holy Communion was a major annual event in the neighborhood. Joey's had been recorded by his father with his new 8 millimeter Bell and Howell home movie camera, and to Joey's embarrassment the film was shown at every family gathering. There Joey was, in glorious Technicolor, his tight white poplin pants bulging, walking carefully, thanking God that wool pants did not come in white. He wore a crisp white shirt that was too tight around the collar, and a shiny plain yellow tie. The whole neighborhood had turned out for the ceremony, even Nonna and a disapproving Nonno Beppino. The bishop himself, a red-faced, smiling man with white hair and kind eyes, had come to preside at the service. This bishop was later made a cardinal, and on his way by ship to Rome had contracted gangrene, and despite being put to bed in the Vatican with the venerated arm of a saint beside him, died in agony. But on that spring day three years ago, he moved through the crowd in his splendid white and gold embroidered robes with a tall golden miter on his head, carrying a golden shepherd's crook that flashed reflections of the bright sun into the eyes of the onlookers, making tiny Signs of the Cross to the applauding crowd. Behind the bishop came Father Louis and his altar boys, then several acolytes in black, two of them swinging golden censers giving off great billows of pungent smoke that smelled like the sweet Marsala wine that Nonna served with her *biscotti*. Then, like a vision of heaven emerging from the smoke, came the long line of angelic kids in their white shirts, pants, and dresses, their hands clasped in prayer, glancing shyly at the camera, shuffling into the sweltering church.

Joey remembered his acute discomfort when everyone had managed to squeeze inside the little church, every seat and inch of aisle filled. The mass was inordinately long, and Joey's anus was itching something fierce. Beside him, poor Benita began to whimper. She whispered that she had to pee. Soon she got up and ran crying from the church, condemned to another eon of purgatory by the weakness of her bladder.

Finally the bishop came forward carrying the chalice, and the kids rose and went single file to receive their First Holy Communion. Father Louis had rehearsed them in every part of the ritual, telling them that the honor of the parish was riding on their performance. He had stressed that under no circumstance should they ever chew the host, this being an injury to the body of Christ, and instead must allow it to melt on their tongues. At the altar rail, Joey stuck out his tongue and looked up at the bishop, who blinked both kind eyes to remind Joey he should keep his own eyes closed as the wafer entered, the better to savor the pure spirituality of the moment. As Joey made his way back to his seat, he could see the beaming faces of his parents and grandparents, aunts, uncles, cousins, and neighbors. It gave him secret satisfaction that under their very gaze he was slowly, defiantly, chewing the host. With any luck, he thought, it might count as a mortal sin and he'd be done with that dumb black armband once and for all.

All this had happened three years ago. Now that he was ten, Joey was to go through the ceremony again, this time to be confirmed in the faith. The procession was just as before, except led by a new bishop. Father Louis, now three years older and more bitter than ever, followed with the acolytes and the billowing smoke. The younger children in white receiving their First Holy Communion were next, followed at last by those being confirmed, who were dressed in red robes. Joey found himself enjoying this ceremony much more than the first. He liked the feeling of seniority, as well as the flashy red robe, beneath whose voluminous folds he wore comfortable pants. Most of all, he had enjoyed the chance to choose a confirmation name from the lengthy list of saints, the selection being meant to signify a commitment to follow the saint's example in a particular arena of spiritual endeavor. For Joey, the philosophical implications of this choice were less important than the opportunity to compensate for his lackluster middle name, Lawrence, inherited from his Nonno Lorenzo, by choosing a name with more zest and dash. There was, alas, no saint Rigoletto, but his eye fell on the name Aloysius. It had quite a ring to it, he thought, Joey Lawrence Aloysius. Better yet, he noticed that Aloysius was the patron saint of youth, so that choosing him implied no particular commitment, in the way that choosing St. Francis, for example, might imply a commitment to becoming a veterinarian.

Once confirmed and a full-fledged member of the parish, Joey soon found he was required to participate in celebrations of the entire liturgical calendar. Some were fun, like the procession in which the statue of the Virgin Mary was carried through the streets, or the day the animals of the neighborhood were brought to the church to be blessed, even Nonna's canary Lucia, though it caught a cold in the course of the ritual and was found dead in its cage the next day. To Joey's mind, the most grotesque ritual was held on Black Friday, when everyone lined up to kiss the wounds on the plaster statue of Christ. In the weeks that followed, a flu epidemic swept the neighborhood, and so Joey learned that good intentions do not always produce good outcomes.

Another result of having been confirmed was that Joey went, as was the tradition in the parish, into instruction to become an altar boy. Bruno had been an altar boy for years, and encouraged Joey by telling him there were all kinds of benefits, like marching in processions, and serving at weddings where there were often generous tips for the boys and lots of free food after.

So early on a Saturday morning, he joined his cousin Peter, his schoolmate Big Paulie, the evil Rex, and a few others sitting in the front pew of the church. They were all bundled in heavy coats because the weather had turned cold again, and the church was freezing because Father Louis was too stingy to heat the place except on Sundays. They could hear the priest bustling about in the vestry and, after a long wait, Rex grabbed Joey's hat from his hand and threw it up on the altar. Joey lurched forward to retrieve it just as a furious Father Louis rushed in and slapped him so hard across the face that he fell down and knocked over the bells on the altar steps. In a rage at this injustice, Joey ran from the church, refused to attend any further instruction, and never did become an altar boy, a decision made easier by the vigorous support of his socialist grandfather.

His refusal to serve, however, did not absolve him from being the symbolic representative of his entire family every Sunday for years after, the others being excused by their hard work during the week and because Sunday morning was the only time his parents could be alone to make love.

11 BREAD AND MILK

On the way home from church every Sunday, Joey had two chores: to buy freshly baked bread for his own family and for his grandparents, and to buy a quart of milk since the milkman didn't deliver on weekends. But first, as soon as Mass ended, he always ran a few doors down from Saint Michael's to visit his mother's grandfather, Great-Grandfather BisNonno Pucci, who lived with his senile and bedridden Great-Aunt Delia.

BisNonno Pucci was an elfin, ever-smiling man who always wore a battered slouch hat and had an old pipe permanently clenched in his teeth. In this pipe there was a perpetual fire, a mass of tobacco burning like a molten ingot in a tiny Bessemer furnace. He often smoked the surplus ends of Italian cigars donated by everyone who knew him, but when he had consumed his supply of cigar butts, he smoked a foul-smelling pure Turkish tobacco called *La Turca*. You could always tell when BisNonno Pucci had visited because the odor of *La Turca* lingered in the house for weeks.

Everyone believed the old man was a shaman with curative powers. Mother swore that when she was little she had a mole on her hand, and BisNonno had rubbed it with a piece of salt pork while muttering an incantation. He then carried the magical pork on the trolley out to the far western farmlands, buried it in a place his mother would never pass, and within a week the mole disappeared forever. More famous was the time when Great-Aunt Delia had suddenly died and BisNonno Pucci had beaten a raw egg and slid it into her mouth, clapped her on the back, and revived her. A miracle!

BisNonno was always glad to see Joey, and Joey loved his visits because BisNonno told him old Italian fairy tales he had learned as a boy in Florence, dark stories full of violence and gore. On this particular Sunday in early spring, he regaled Joey with the saga of the One-Handed Murderer, a story about a princess who had once cut off the hand of a burglar and was hounded by him for years until he finally invaded her chamber and demanded that she bring him a towel because he was going to cut her throat and wanted to wipe the blood from his one good hand afterward. She pretended to obey, but wrapped a pistol inside the towel and shot him through the heart.

This story, like all the others, was told in the bedroom of Great-Aunt Delia, who sat propped up on pillows and listened with childlike delight. BisNonno acted it out with dramatic gestures, recreating the voice of each character, and building it to a spine-tingling climax. Great-Aunt Delia squealed and clapped her hands at the end.

After his visit with BisNonno Pucci and Great-Aunt Delia, smelling of *La Turca*, Joey hurried two blocks down Oakley Avenue to buy fresh bread at Fontana's Bakery, a wondrous place that was full of the most wonderful smells. There was sawdust on the floor and glass cases full of several kinds of rolls, *biscotti*, pastries like thick Napoleans, cakes, and myriad cookies. Behind the counter were big wooden bins filled with breads of all sizes and shapes, fat oblong ones, big round ones, long thin ones, even little pencil-sized sticks, all with the crisp crust of real unsalted Tuscan bread. Joey's family always got a *ciabatta*, an old shoe, a long, fat oblong bread, hard and heavy. Once, when his mother had been overcome by a rare fit of anger, she had thrown one of these big breads at Joey, who ducked, and it had broken the big kitchen window.

Fontana's had a big white machine that sliced the bread, but his family never wanted it sliced because it got stale too quickly, and the slices from the machine were too thin. Bread, they believed, should be cut very thick just before serving, though Nonno Beppino adhered to the peasant tradition of tearing it from the loaf in hand-sized chunks. Joey bought, as usual, two loaves for his parents and two for Nonno and Nonna. The baker rolled each loaf up in a sheet of crisp white paper and sealed it with a strip of white tape. Joey also got a *Bucellato*, a Tuscan style of *Pandolce*, the sweet dark anise-flavored bread filled with bits of candied fruit, raisins, and almonds that Fontana made only on Sundays. When toasted for breakfast, it released an aroma that sweetened the air of the whole house.

PANDOLCE ALL'ITALIANA

1 cup butter
1 cup sugar
1 tsp vanilla
2 cups sifted flour
6 eggs
¼ cup candied citron
¼ cup chopped almonds
¼ cup candied orange peel
¼ cup sultanas

Cream butter in a warm bowl, add sugar gradually and beat mixture until light and creamy. Add vanilla and two eggs at a time, beating mixture after each addition; stir in flour. Fold in nuts and fruit. Place in a long, narrow, buttered pan, and bake in a hot oven at 375° for about 45 minutes.

Besides the Sunday bread, Joey was also to buy milk. His folks assumed he would buy the milk at Zanardo's market across the street from Fontana's bakery. Zanardo's market was a cornucopia that overflowed onto the sidewalk, with rows of fruits and vegetables, hanging strings of garlic and dried peppers, and straw baskets full of pungent white slabs of *bacallá*, dried cod, under the green roll-up awning. Inside, the shelves were packed to overflowing with five-gallon cans of olive oil, jars of olives, capers, bins full of every kind of pasta imaginable, huge glass cylinders of *antipasti*, oddly shaped boxes of *panetone*, wicker-covered bottles of Chianti, and fascinating little boxes of the candy called *Torrone* with baroque pictures of the Leaning Tower of Pisa and other wonders of the Old World. Hanging from Zanardo's ceiling was a forest of tied-up salami, chains of sausage, and that ultimate Tuscan staple, bulky *prosciutti*, whole shanks of cured ham. Almost every family in Tuscany made its own particular *prosciutto*, the flavor of each being determined not only by the method of curing, but also by the food given the pig during its lifetime. As a girl in Tuscany, Nonna Augusta had fed her family's pigs huge, overgrown zucchini, and the delicate flavor of the squash lingered in the *prosciutto* they produced. When visitors come into a household in Tuscany or on the West Side, three things appear immediately on the table: a bottle of local wine, a loaf of fresh crusty bread, and a platter of the *prosciutto della casa* sliced so thin you can read a newspaper through it. Though individual families could not keep their own pigs here on the West Side of Chicago, Zanardo raised pigs on a farm in Michigan and made several styles of *prosciutto* for the whole neighborhood.

Some American neighborhoods, like old world villages, are centered around their churches, but the West Side had grown up around Fontana's and Zanardo's. They provided everything needed for a bountiful life. The street between them, filled with the smells of baking bread mixed with the complex odors of olives, meats, fresh fruit, and vegetables, was a veritable banquet. A few deep breaths here could sustain a person for days. In comparison, the drafty, musty little church was almost an afterthought. As Father sometimes said, give a *Toscano* the choice between nourishing his stomach or his soul and there will be little doubt of the outcome.

The neighborhood cared for its own in hard times from birth to death and everything in between. Old man Zanardo and the Fontana Brothers, like Fan and most of the other merchants on the West Side, had extended credit to the neighborhood families and carried them through the Depression, as had Doc Salvia the dentist, Mirabella the doctor who had delivered both Joey and his mother, Silvio the barber, and even Leo Anzilotti, the undertaker. People from the neighborhood, even after they had long since moved away, often came back to get bread from Fontana's and *prosciutto* from Zanardo's, to see Doc Salvia or Doc Mirabella, or get a haircut from Silvio. And they always came back to be buried by Leo Anzilotti.

But as wonderful as Zanardo's market was, Joey didn't buy the Sunday milk there. He went instead to a little place he had discovered a few weeks before. He had been walking on Twenty-fourth Street, a street he seldom visited, when he noticed a sign hanging in the shadows of a gangway between two houses very like his own. He went closer and saw that the sign, in faded and crudely drawn letters, said MILK DEPOT. He climbed down the stairs into the gangway and walked to the back of the house. There, above the door of an enclosed porch just like his own, was another sign, so faded that it was barely legible, again saying MILK DEPOT. He tried the door and it was open.

Inside, a small bell attached to the door with a coiled spring tinkled when he passed through. There was a card table that served as a counter, faded linoleum on the floor, a bare bulb hanging from the ceiling, and an ordinary icebox against one wall. On the icebox was a sign written in a tremulous hand, MILK 25¢ QT. He waited a few minutes, then called, Hello? Anyone here? Soon he saw a figure stirring inside the house, and an impossibly old woman appeared through the kitchen door. She was stooped so low he could not see her face, only the great tufts of white hair growing from her ears so thick that he wondered if she could hear at all. She didn't speak or raise her head. In a loud voice he said, I'd like a quart of milk. Still without looking at him, she opened the icebox with great deliberation, her arthritic fingers bulging at the joints, removed a bottle, wiped off the top, and put it on the table. Joey gave her a quarter. Her hand shook as she took it, opened a small metal box on the card table, and dropped it inside. The coins rattled as she carefully closed the lid. Then she turned and shuffled back into the darkness of the house. On subsequent visits, the old woman was sometimes replaced by an even older man, so pale that his skin seemed transparent, but the ritual was always the same, and Joey never heard either of them speak.

Milk here cost five cents more than at Zanardo's, and Joey understood that this extra five cents represented the profit and probably the major livelihood of the two old people. He imagined that the Milk Depot was the focus of their lives, the one thing that gave meaning and purpose to their silent existence. He felt a solemn responsibility to buy milk from them and for the rest of his life had a special feeling for the little mom and pop stores that became increasingly rare as the years passed.

The first time Joey bought milk at the Milk Depot, his mother noticed the change he returned to her was five cents short. He couldn't bring himself to tell her why. He knew that money was precious, and he couldn't ask his parents to subsidize his private charity. He was also afraid that if he did explain, his mother would order him to stop going to the Depot, and if that happened he would be terribly disappointed in her. He was also, for some reason, embarrassed by his sense of obligation to the old couple. So he told his mother that he must have dropped the nickel on his way back from the store. Suspecting that he was lying and had spent the nickel on candy, his mother insisted that he go back and look for it.

For a long time that Sunday evening, Joey walked up and down Oakley Avenue, staring at the ground, looking intently for a nickel that he knew did not exist. At last he went home and with real shame reported that he had not found it. After that, he saved what he could to buy milk at the Milk Depot, and once his coffee run was established he used some of his profits to visit more often, buying milk he sometimes gave away to friends. He did this all that spring, until one day the sign was gone, the porch and house were dark, and the door was boarded shut. He knocked, and peered inside, but saw no sign of life. Not wanting to know what had happened, he never went back.

12 MUSEUM DREAMS

JOEY WENT TO BED RIGHT AFTER THE LAST OF THE TELEVISION PROGRAMS. His mother came in to make sure he said his nightly prayer. She knelt beside him and together they murmured, Now I lay me down to sleep, I pray the Lord my soul to keep, but if I die before I wake, I pray the Lord my soul to take. The prayer seemed to Joey full of dark forebodings. Mother kissed him and tucked him in and he lay there, quite still, imagining death, and listening to the murmur of his parent's voices.

On some nights their voices would grow loud in argument, though his mother would usually say, The boy can hear us, and they would stop. But tonight the argument was especially heated, and Joey heard them go outside. He listened a few minutes to their faint, angry voices, then got up and went to the kitchen window. Faintly, he could see his mother and father face to face in the back yard, speaking through clenched teeth in subdued but furious tones, his mother punctuating her words with shakes of her head, his father with his hands on his hips. Joey was gripped with a deep, sinking coldness in the pit of his stomach. He got the flashlight from the tool drawer, opened the back door and called out through tears, Don't argue, please, come in, stop arguing, and his parents looked into the beam of his light like deer caught in the headlights of a car.

They had come in and reassured him, it was just a disagreement, nothing to worry about. They took him into his room and put him back to bed. Mother kissed him lightly and Father squeezed his arm, then they turned out the light. Soon he heard them in their own room, murmuring without anger. Then it was quiet, and Joey waited for the moment of sleep to come, and eventually it did. The dreams followed.

Most of Joey's dreams were in Technicolor. On this night, brightly colored mummies rose up out of grand pianos and chased him, trundling from side to side in their gilded cases. Joey ran from them, that terrible slow-motion run, barely making any headway despite desperate effort, through a strange and forbidding landscape. When the draft from the open back door woke his parents later that night, they found Joey's room empty. A frantic search found him wandering two blocks away, barefoot, still sound asleep. Don't wake him up, his mother said. If you wake up a sleepwalker they could go crazy or even die. So Joey was guided gently back to his bed, still asleep.

When he recounted the dream in the morning, his mother blamed it on their recent Sunday outing to the Field Museum of Natural History and its Egyptian Room with rows and rows of mummies in their cases. I knew you shouldn't have taken him in there, she said to Father. All those dead people, he'll probably have nightmares for life.

But Joey was hooked on the Field Museum, with its huge

dinosaur skeletons in the main hall, and begged to go back, promising even to forgo the mummies. His mother, however, had a better idea. That Sunday the family went instead to the Museum of Science and Industry. As they walked toward the grand edifice in Jackson Park, Mother explained that it had been built for the Columbian Exposition of 1893. Joey was fascinated by the huge stone women that held up the porches on either side of the main building. Mother told him these were called caryatids, and Joey was amazed again at how smart she was. Not to be outdone, Father pointed at the lagoon behind the building and whispered, That's where Leopold and Loeb dumped the typewriter they used to write the ransom note when they killed little Bobbie Franks. Somehow Joey was not surprised that his father knew this.

Inside the great entry hall, Joey was hypnotized by the pendulum that hung from the dome of the rotunda, six stories above floor level, slowly tracing the rotation of the earth. On all sides, hallways beckoned that led to various worlds of exploration. In the wing called THE BODY there was a human heart you could walk through, passing from one ventricle into the other while the lighting changed from blue to red and a deep pumping sound shook the floor. And in the wing called NATURE there was a huge Van de Graf generator, a tall black column topped by a shiny silver ball, right out of Flash Gordon, that rumbled for a while, then unleashed a tremendous bolt of lightning that blew up a little model wooden house. In hall after hall, there were contraptions and exhibits like a working farm, whispering chambers, a row of developing fetuses in glass jars, and other wonders.

As exciting as all these exhibits were, they were for Joey only the setting for the real jewel of the museum, the coal mine. As soon as they had come into the museum, Father had gone straight to the ticket booth and had gotten their tickets. As their assigned time to enter the mine neared, they climbed the metal stairs high above the main hall and waited on a small landing with an open grillwork floor. There Joey could look up at the elevator tower that reached to the very ceiling of the museum, from which a cable ran down onto the enormous drum of a huge engine below. The engine's whistle blew a deafening blast, and the drum started to turn. Soon a real mine elevator cage rose to meet them. The attendant slid open the metal door and they shuffled inside, packed cheek by jowl with all kinds of people.

After the attendant made a brief speech about safety, of which Joey heard not a word, the door banged shut and the car was lowered deep into a real mine where real miners with lights on their hats demonstrated long drills that bored holes for blasting, and huge digging machines that roared briefly to life and transported chunks of real coal on conveyor belts. Joey moved wide-eyed from tunnel to tunnel and machine to machine, and sat at last on a bench in a small room where the tour climaxed with an explosion of mine gas inside a glass-walled box.

Outside again, in the bright sunshine, they ate their bag lunch in the park. Joey couldn't stop talking about the coal mine. He begged to go into it again on his own, and Father got him a ticket. At 1:55 sharp, Joey breathlessly climbed the stairs, all by himself, and managed to stand in the very front of the elevator cage next to the door. Joey was pressed beside a black boy who looked a little like Booker T. In spite of himself, Joey stared at the black boy, as if this was his chance to examine Booker T without the intervening rusty bars and grimy factory windows. The boy stared back, seeming just as interested in Joey, and their eyes locked. Joey raised his hand and the boy raised his in response. Just then the elevator lurched and the two boys were pushed against one another, instinctively grasping each other's hands for support. The boy was wide-eyed. It was perhaps the first time he had touched white skin. The boy's mother jerked him away and hissed, What you doin', James? Don't be touchin' strange people. Joey glanced up at her, but she stared resolutely straight ahead. Joey had been told by other neighborhood kids that Negroes smelled bad, but he enjoyed her lavender perfume, strong and sweet, and the boy smelled of fresh soap.

It was on this second trip into the mine, when the surprise had worn off and he was able to pay attention to details, that Joey realized the wall of the elevator shaft was actually a conveyor belt that moved to create the illusion of a long descent, that the miners were in fact bored old men who recited their speeches mechanically, that the chunks of coal were fakes permanently affixed to the conveyor belts, and that the whole mine was in the museum's basement, just three stories beneath the starting point. Some boys might have been disillusioned by these discoveries, but Joey was even more fascinated by the mechanics of the illusion than if things had been as they seemed.

For many nights thereafter, the clumsy mummies of Joey's earlier dreams were replaced by coal-digging machines with claws that scuttled after him like huge metal crabs, and crazed old miners wielding long drills.

13 THE SAUCE WARS

The three main family holidays, Thanksgiving, Christmas, and Easter, were occasions for huge gatherings, a tradition brought from the old country when people gathered from various Tuscan towns to visit and exchange gifts, news, introduce newborns, mourn the recently dead, and, most of all, to eat, and to eat, and to eat again. Each gathering was preceded by days of continuous cooking in all the far-flung kitchens of the family, the results borne in huge pots, platters, and bowls covered with aluminum foil in the back seats of cars, all converging on the groaning board of one of the family homes, although never had one of these gatherings been held in their basement flat, which could not have held everyone, the great-grandparents, grandparents, parents, aunts, uncles, and cousins to the third power, a mob of more than thirty.

In a rotation determined by long-standing tradition, Thanksgiving was always upstairs at Nonna Augusta's, and Christmas was in the suburbs with Nonna Severina. Easter, however, was a moveable feast and was held at whichever of the family houses was new, or in which there had recently been a marriage, birth, or death that needed to be consecrated, celebrated, or mourned. This spring, the Easter dinner was held at his Uncle Louis' new house in the suburbs, a house built specifically to accommodate his family, plus an extra room and bath to accommodate Nonna Severina whenever she might join them after the eventual death of Nonno Lorenzo. The tradition of taking surviving parents into the home had been brought over from Italy, where nursing homes would have been considered barbaric, and almost every home on the West Side housed three, sometimes four, generations, and houses were chosen and built with this eventuality in mind.

This Easter Sunday was one of the rare days that Joey's parents went to 10 o'clock Mass with him and suffered the knee-numbing length of the High Mass. After they had lit candles to the repose of various souls, they rushed home and loaded the Packard for the trip to Uncle Louis' house, Joey sharing the back seat with their contributions to the feast, several platters and bowls tightly covered by aluminum foil. The sky was a deep blue after months of overcast. Looking out the back window as they drove out of the city and into the wooded suburbs, it seemed to Joey that everything was in sharp focus, as if the smudged lens of winter had been polished clean.

They arrived by noon and carried their offerings inside. Most of the other women had arrived earlier to help with preparations. Already, every table in the house was covered with little bowls and plates full of green, black, and stuffed olives, nuts, raisins, dates, chocolates, Hershey's kisses, the colorful boxes of *Torrone*, and special miniature Easter baskets filled with white, pink, and pale blue Jordan almonds. Despite the warning of mothers to their children and husbands not to spoil their appetites, handful after handful of these delicacies were immediately consumed.

By one o'clock, the last guest, the venerable BisNonno Pucci, arrived and was forcibly restrained from lighting his pipe. The kids were ushered into the back yard for an Easter egg hunt, for which Joey considered himself too grown up, though he allowed himself to be persuaded to join in and found the most eggs. After the hunt, the men lit cigarettes and gathered like hunters around a campfire to watch a Bears game on Uncle Louis' little Zenith television, while all the women insisted on helping in the kitchen even though there wasn't room for all of them, and the kids ran around and hid in bedrooms and played with the toys of the host children, cousins Randy and Darryl. Joey, as usual, snuck off on his own secret raid to search in dresser drawers and the backs of closets.

By two o'clock the antipasto was brought out, large trays of stuffed celery and mushrooms, green onions, olives, deviled eggs, little sausages, melon balls wrapped in *prosciutto*, sliced salami, *mortadella* and *capicollo*, pickled peppers and wrinkled *pepperoncini*, slabs of Swiss, cheddar, Fontina, and Gorgonzola cheeses, marinated artichoke hearts, stalks of fennel in olive oil and black pepper, and whatever else had been available at Zanardo's market. Supreme amidst this bounty were plate upon plate of the beloved little *crostini*, toasted rounds of Italian bread covered with finely ground, sautéed chicken livers and capers, especially delicious the way Joey's Nonna Severina made them.

CROSTINI ALLA NONNA SEVERINA

1 lb fresh chicken livers

¾ cup or so olive oil

1 bunch Italian parsley, chopped fine

1 medium yellow onion, chopped fine

1 clove garlic, chopped fine (optional)

3 TB water

6 oz. canned tomato sauce

½ cup butter

2 oz. capers, rinsed and chopped fine

5 anchovy filets (optional)

Fresh ground black pepper

2 or more baguettes cut in ¾" slices and toasted

Wash the livers and drain dry. Heat the oil and butter over medium heat in a sauté pan and brown the livers, being careful not to burn them. Put the livers aside and sauté the parsley, onion, and garlic (if you choose to use it), adding 3 TB of water and cooking down until the onions are translucent. Avoid burning or even browning the onions and parsley. Then add the tomato sauce and cook at low heat for 12 minutes. Meanwhile, grind the chicken liver in a grinder or food processor. Add them to the pan and heat for 15 minutes more, thinning with butter if necessary. Halfway through this cooking, add the thoroughly rinsed, chopped capers. If you choose to use the anchovy, break the filets up and add just before serving. This sauce will be very thick. Nonna made it very smooth, but some like it chunky, chopping the ingredients more coarsely. To serve, cut rounds of Italian bread about ¾" thick and toast, then spread the sauce on thick. Serve warm as soon as possible, especially if anchovy has been used. As an appetizer, serves 8 Italians or 12 non-Italians.

The main meal began around two-thirty and lasted until the springtime sun set about three hours later. Everyone was called to the table, the seating established by tradition, BisNonno Pucci at the head and Nonno Beppino at the foot. The chairs nearest the kitchen were always reserved for the women of the house, though they never actually sat down until after the dessert was served. The children were happily consigned to card tables set up wherever there was room, and the eldest kids were enjoined to set a good example. Full tumblers of homemade wine were poured from gallon jugs that were kept ready-to-hand on the floor beside both Nonnos. The wine was diluted with water for children and older people with special conditions. In a surprisingly short time, the jugs had to be refilled from the big, round, straw-covered carboys in the basement.

In Joey's family no grace was said, as both Nonnos were devout socialists, so as soon as everyone was seated the talking began in earnest. The conversation was lively and varied: news was exchanged concerning the far-flung network of the family, reaching to fourth and fifth cousins in other cities and countries; arguments about politics, sports, and religion raged, memories were revived, advice was too freely given. Throughout, the unspoken rule for all Italian dinner conversations was strictly observed: each person was allowed to talk only to those sitting furthest away from them, so the din soon reached a level at which permanent hearing damage was a real possibility.

Into this roaring torrent of words floated great bowls and platters of food. The soup came first, *Tortellini in Brodo* at Thanksgiving and Easter, *Minestrone* at Christmas. The older people broke pieces of bread into their soup and sprinkled it with heaps of freshly grated *Parmesano Reggiano*, *Romano*, and *Pecorino* cheeses. The gusto with which the soup was inhaled produced a great symphony of slurping. After the soup came several pastas, always including simple spaghetti with meatballs, *mostaciolli* in meat sauce, and *ravioli* filled with meat, spinach and cheese, as well as *tortellini* or even *gnocchi*, all served with bowls of freshly grated cheeses. Special orders of plain spaghetti with butter and cheese were available for the faint of heart, but meat sauce remained the foundation of most dishes. Each grandmother had her own version of meat sauce, though it was understood that no comparisons or preferences between them were to be even whispered, as this was the one thing that could rip asunder the fabric of the family. Nevertheless, an undeclared sauce war was waged in the secret heart of every member of the family. Nonna Severina's sauce was hearty and thick, best when mixed generously into the pasta.

SALSA DI CARNE ALLA NONNA SEVERINA
½ lb each of veal and pork, ground
1 yellow onion, chopped
1 cup red wine
1 small can tomatoes
¼ cup olive oil
3 tbsp Italian parsley, minced
salt and pepper
pinch of basil and oregano

Brown meat and onion in hot olive oil. Heat tomatoes and wine to boiling point, add to meat with parsley and seasonings. Simmer for 30 minutes or more. Serves eight, depending on how liberally it is applied to the pasta.

Nonna Augusta's sauce, on the other hand, was more subtle, thinner and sweeter, a good basis for other dishes like *Vitello alla Parmigiana.*

SALSA DI CARNE ALLA NONNA AUGUSTA
1 clove garlic
2 lbs twice-ground beef
2 yellow onions, minced
2 small cans tomato puree
6 cups water
3 bay leaves
1 tsp fennel seed
2 tblsps sugar

½ cup olive oil
salt and pepper
pinch of basil and oregano

Brown garlic, meat and onion in hot olive oil, remove garlic. Add tomato puree, water, bay leaves, sugar and other seasonings. Simmer for 1 hour or more. Serves eight.

Though each member of the family harbored a secret preference for one of these sauces over the other, there was one dish on which there was universal accord. Nonna Severina was the undisputed queen of meatballs, and even Nonna Augusta declined to contest her superiority in that arena. As a gesture of conciliation at gatherings where both sides of the family were present, however, Nonna Severina's meatballs were served with Nonna Augusta's sauce.

MEATBALLS (POLPETTONI DI BUE) ALLA NONNA SEVERINA

1 lb. coarsely ground round steak
4 tbsp Italian parsley, chopped
2 eggs, beaten
salt and pepper
½ cup breadcrumbs
¼ cup milk
6 tblsp Parmesan cheese, grated
Oregano and marjoram
Olive Oil
2 cups Tomato sauce

Mix all ingredients except tomato sauce thoroughly; shape into balls the size of small oranges. Brown in hot olive oil, add to tomato sauce and simmer 30 minutes.

The pasta course signaled the end of the foreplay, and now the meal entered its most serious phase with the appearance of the meats, which in the old country were expensive treats reserved for special occasions like these. To set the stage for the meats, salads and various *contorni* were laid out, the selection depending on the season. There were usually mixed lettuces and sliced tomatoes and onions in vinaigrette, fresh green beans with slivered almonds, spinach sautéed in olive oil with garlic, fresh peas with baby onions, bean salad with chick peas, mashed potatoes with gravy, and more. All these, along with an infinite supply of warm Tuscan bread and butter, remained available throughout the meal. Bread was used as an essential utensil, and even as an adult Joey was unable to eat without it.

Traditional Italian main dishes were strictly the province of the Nonnas, but certain side dishes had, over the years, become the prerogative of one or another of the younger women in the family. Aunt Diana came to be the main source of candied yams with melted marshmallow topping, though this was often forgotten in the oven when the meal was finally served. Joey's mother, who thought of herself as a modern American cook, supplied non-Italian components like lime Jello molded with mandarin oranges, which, in the spirit of ecumenism, was tolerated, albeit condescendingly.

When the various side dishes were laid, the chicken appeared, roasted with fresh sage, and crusty potatoes quartered and roasted in the pan. Only after the chicken was devoured did the roasts arrive. The roast course usually consisted of two choices. One favorite was roast veal rubbed with olive oil and larded with slivers of garlic, another was roast leg of lamb with peas, yet another, pot roast of beef cooked in white wine. All these had the crucial advantage of being prepared in advance and holding well until it was time to serve, unlike grilled or sautéed meats, which were generally avoided at these huge gatherings.

After the roast, as the sun was beginning to set, it was time for the desserts. Sadly, the family avoided the chestnut dishes that were common in the area of Tuscany from which they came, as chestnuts gave both Nonnos terrible heartburn. But a splendid array of desserts were always served, made in advance and held for service in the *refridgidere*, or even on the back porch in cold weather. These most often took the form of puddings like *Zuppa Inglise*, *tiramisu*, almond rice pudding, lemon custard, pears in wine, and sweet *ricotta* with pineapple chunks. Aunt Mary, who was Hungarian and the only non-Italian in the family, was the acknowledged master baker and provided all manner of cakes and cookies. Joey's mother, the modern American cook, was the sole supplier of a radically non-Italian but nevertheless favorite dessert called simply The Green Stuff.

MOTHER'S GREEN STUFF

The Shell: Roll 18 Graham crackers until fine, add ½ cup sugar and 1/3 cup melted butter. Toss with a fork and press into pie tins or a large flat baking dish. Reserve some for topping. Chill while making the filling.

The Filling: Add 3 oz. Lime Jello mix to 1 cup boiling water, let it cool but not set. Blend 8 oz. cream cheese with ¾ cup sugar until very smooth and creamy. In a chilled bowl, add cool Jello and 1 can of chilled Milnot or Evaporated Milk, and whip all with chilled beaters until stiff. Pour into chilled shells and return to refrigerator until served. Sprinkle with excess Graham cracker crumbs.

After the main desserts had been passed, the coffee was served along with platters of almond crescents, *biscotti*, and almond macaroons so hard you had to hold them down in the coffee until they were soft enough to chew. There were also *torroni, cannoloni*, anise slices, cream puffs, and rum cake. Liqueurs like *Amaretto, Anisette, Moscato Passato, Vin Santo*, or *Strega* were sipped or added to coffee. Lastly, to clean the palate, there was *spumoni* or *gelato* in several flavors.

The men now retreated to the living room, belts were loosened, gas not so politely passed, cigarettes, cigars, and pipes lit, though BisNonno was banished to the porch, where the odor of his *La Turca* could dissipate harmlessly. The heaviness of the meal finally brought the level of discourse down to a satisfied murmur while the women of the house worked to clear the table.

This interval lasted two or three hours, during which the women prepared the supper. At about eight o'clock, with much protest, the men would heave themselves up from the sofa, chair, or floor and stagger to the table for an encore that always included at least two new dishes, perhaps spaghetti with sweet fennel sausage, chicken *cacciatore*, or *vitello marsala*. Even while swearing that it was impossible to eat more, everyone soon found their second wind and consumed nearly as much again as they had in the afternoon.

Shortly after this second meal, the parting ritual began. What Joey called the Long Italian Goodbye could last an hour or more as the departing guests moved through a series of steps prescribed by tradition. In the first stage, all the women crowded into the dining room and kitchen to help clean up, though the women of the host house protested, *lasci, lasci, noi lo faremo di mattina*, leave it, leave it, we'll do it in the morning, though everyone knew they would stay up all night if necessary until the kitchen shone and every pot, pan, plate, glass, and fork was back in its place. Meanwhile, the men talked in the living room, or, in good weather, went outside to have a last smoke while looking under the hoods of one another's cars. In stage two, the bowls, platters, serving spoons, and children brought by guests were retrieved and coats were put on. Stage three was of indeterminate length as guests moved to the door, where bundles of leftovers wrapped in aluminum foil were distributed: here, take this, no, please, we have so much, everyone is getting some, we really don't have room, here, just in case. This last, Just in case, was the final, irrefutable argument that governed much of family life. Joey wondered what tragedy might befall them on the way home that would require a bowl of meatballs, but he assumed it was the same sort of emergency that made it important to always wear clean underwear and, as he now well understood, clean socks.

Laden with their provisions, Joey and his folks were shepherded out of the house by Nonna, Uncle Louis, Aunt Mary, and cousins Randy and Darryl. This crowd moved a few feet out onto the steps, talked, went down the steps, talked, got to the sidewalk, talked, and then got to the car, where they opened whole new subjects for discussion. At last Joey and his folks got into the car and Father started the engine. Windows were rolled down for repeated farewells, kisses, and waves. At last they pulled away. After a few blocks, Father leaned far to one side and an enormous rumble ensued. He cried, Oh God, I let a wet one!

Mother cried, Dino! Open the window, for God's sake!

Joey laughed, sitting in back watching over the plates and bowls of leftovers, happily anticipating days of tasty respite from his mother's Lipton's Noodle Soup.

14 RIVERVIEW

ONE SUNDAY, A MONTH AFTER THE EASTER DINNER, Joey got home after church and delivered his grandparents' share of the bread, *buccelato*, and milk. Downstairs, his parents were preparing for the weekly family outing. This Sunday morning ritual was as unchanging as the Mass. Right after a late breakfast, Father went out to the garage and did whatever maintenance the Packard required. Today, Joey helped him change the oil. Father scooted under the car on his creeper and Joey handed him wrenches and other tools like an operating room nurse. Joey loved these sessions and was soon able to anticipate whatever tools Father needed without being asked. The love of machines and the deep understanding of how they functioned that Joey absorbed from his father on these Sunday mornings never left him, and in later life he had an almost mystical rapport with machinery of all kinds.

When the car had been serviced, Joey and Father would get it washed. The carwash on Cermak Road advertised itself as AUTOMATIC, meaning that the car was pulled by a chain attached to an overhead conveyor through a gauntlet of men, some at the sides with large brushes, some on a walkway above with brushes attached to long wands, and some in a pit beneath the car, washing the bumpers and tires. The men all wore long rubber aprons, boots, and gloves, just like Luther and the other men in the electroplating factory, and like them, all were black. Joey asked his father about this, and his father replied matter-of-factly, This is the kind of job that niggers do, like down at the plant, the niggers are the day laborers who do the sweeping and move material, though a few have worked their way up to running machines, and they're damn good workers, better than some of the whites.

Back home, after the car was shined and swept, the Sunday ritual continued. Father, Mother, Joey, Nonno, and Nonna would squeeze in and drive to visit one of the relatives who had managed to move out of the city to one of the western suburbs like Brookfield, LaGrange, or North Riverside. As part of these Sunday visits, Joey and Father and Mother would drive around the wonderful wooded suburban neighborhoods looking at houses, dreaming of the day when they too could escape the city and their basement flat.

This particular Sunday, however, was to be something very special. It was Memorial Day weekend, the traditional opening of the grand amusement park called Riverview, and four of the neighborhood families were going together. Joey was overjoyed. Riverview Park was the Promised Land, the Holy Grail for three generations of neighborhood children, parents, and grandparents before them. Riverview was a living chronicle of the lives of people on the West Side. They were taken there when they were kids, went there on dates when they were older, went as couples when they were married and took kids of their own, and finally went as oldsters sitting quietly on shaded benches, doling out dimes and quarters to the grandchildren who came running to them between rides. Each family had its own cycle of attendance that measured the passage of the generations since the family had arrived in America, most having been swept across the sea as youngsters to find Riverview Park waiting, surpassing anything the old country had to offer.

A trip to Riverview was anticipated for weeks, and in many ways these idylls of anticipation were the most delicious part of the experience. Like master chefs planning the courses of a great meal, the kids gathered to make elaborate plans about the exact sequence in which the rides would be taken. The group included Bruno, Big Paulie, Joey's fourth cousins Arlene and Geraldine, and best of all, Peter and Benita. They discussed and argued about it for days. The main consideration was the relative scariness of the rides. As mountaineers rated the difficulty of the world's peaks, so there was an accepted hierarchy to the rides at Riverview, and you could place yourself within the pecking order of the neighborhood according to the scariest ride you had so far mastered. During the weeks leading up to a visit, each kid considered which of the rides not yet attempted might be conquered on this trip, and dares and double-dares were made. The discussions continued in the car on the way to the park itself. By the time the gates were reached and the group joined the tremendous throng of humanity pushing through the turnstiles, Joey and the others could barely contain their excitement.

There were four rules universally enforced by all parents on a trip to Riverview. Always stay where I can see you, Don't talk to strangers, Don't eat anything you find, and most of all, No Games. The games were the real money-makers at the park, and you could spend enormous sums trying to get a ring around the neck of a Coke bottle, to get a tossed nickel to stay in a dish, or any of a hundred other challenges that looked easy but were nearly impossible. Even if you won, as the mothers always pointed out, the prizes were not worth what you had spent.

There was one game that gave no prizes as such, and was so popular there were two of them in different parts of the park. The banner above these games said DUNK THE NIGGER. The game was simple. A black man dressed in long rubber overalls sat on a small seat from which a lever with a target on the end protruded. Below him was a large tank of water with a glass front. With three balls for ten cents, you tried to hit the target, which released the seat so that the black man would fall into the tank with a great splash. The success of this game depended in large measure on the skill of the black man in hurling insults at the white passersby about appearance, physique, clothing, or skill. Hey fatso, he would yell, bet your wife there can throw better'n you. Surprised she lets you out of the house dressed like that. But then she ain't exactly Joan Crawford herself, is she? Thus inflamed, men would hurl balls as fast as the proprietor, a stout white man who looked like Guy Kibee, could supply them. So virulent were the insults hurled by the black men, Joey guessed that they must be paid by the dunk, or perhaps they simply relished the chance to insult white people in relative safety. Though his mother always rushed him past the booth, Joey watched this game with fascination, thinking sometimes of Luther and Booker T behind the bars of the factory, or the black men wielding brushes in the pit at the car wash, all in their own rubber uniforms, and wondered which occupation offered more, or any, chance at dignity. At least, Joey thought, the black men at Riverview were out in the sun, able to speak their mind, and kept cool on hot days.

Despite the fascination of the games, Riverview was really about the rides, and as soon as possible the kids began to follow the menu they had planned. Dismissed out of hand were rides like the Tunnel of Love, the Caterpillar (whose only virtue was that a canvas cover suddenly engulfed you as you went around the slightly hilly track), the carousel, the dark ride called Laff-in-the-Dark, and the huge Ferris Wheel. All these were considered suitable only for the youngest children. For Joey and his gang, the feast began with the slowest and lowest of the thrill rides, those least likely to induce vomiting, which were taken first as appetizers. These included some classics, like the Tilt-O-Whirl. Although it was common at street carnivals, the Tilt-O-Whirl at Riverview had special status because of its great age and obvious decrepitude. It had recently been elevated several notches on the hierarchy of rides when a car broke loose, crashed through the guard rail, and broke someone's collarbone. Indeed, rumors of injury and even death were important factors in establishing the esteem in which any ride was held. Whip-the-Whip, an otherwise boring ride, creaked and groaned so loudly it always seemed a car would break loose and cause havoc among the onlookers. Standing at the railing that surrounded the Whip-the-Whip, in the spot most likely to receive the impact of a runaway car, was considered almost as good as taking the ride itself.

The best of these low-level rides was the Shoot-the-Chutes, which lifted heavy cars seating some forty people to the top of a long water slide, followed by a rapid descent causing a huge plume of water at the bottom, soaking everyone. It was quite refreshing on a hot day, but the mothers always cautioned the children not to get any of the badly polluted water in their mouths or eyes, saying, You don't know what all is in there.

The entrees of the Riverview feast were the exotic high-speed rides, especially the roller coasters, and even here there was an accepted hierarchy. The tamest was the Greyhound, its only special feature being the tunnel at the bottom of the first hill. Next were two similar coasters, the Blue Streak and the Silver Streak, and there was much debate about preferences between these two. There was no disagreement, however, about the pinnacle of the coasters, the Bobs. The Bobs was the fastest, the steepest, and, because of its steeply banked sharp turns, the most bone-jarring, teeth-rattling, kidney-challenging ride in the park. There was argument about whether sitting in the front or the back was the scariest, and opinion was divided between those who preferred the downhill speed of the rear seats and those who preferred the uphill weightlessness of the front seats. No wait was too long to obtain the highly prized front-most or rear-most seats. And care was taken also with seating arrangements, so that the heaviest rider was placed on the inside of the tightest turns so as not to crush his or her seatmate. The slow trip up the first hill, the ratchets banging noisily beneath the car, past the sign that said DO NOT STAND UP, was the most terrifying part of the ride, and it was here that the story was always told of the sailor who ignored the warning and was decapitated.

There was another coaster-like ride that Joey considered the equal of the Bobs, though not everyone agreed. This was the Flying Turns, in which three persons got into a bobsled-like car, lying almost prone atop one another. The car was pulled up the first hill like any other roller coaster, but at the crest it was released to run free, without tracks, in an open-topped tube much like a bobsled run, but with tighter turns. Masters of the ride tried to force the car higher up the tube walls by shifting their bodies in unison in the turns, but the well-worn markings on the floor showed that the path of the car varied little. Still, the illusion of freedom of movement, like the illusion of free will, was thrilling, as was the pressure of Benita's body atop his when Joey managed to arrange the seating so that she was sandwiched between him and Peter. As the car clanked noisily up the first hill,

Joey could feel Benita's hips nestled between his legs, the small of her back against his groin, his arms around her shoulders so that he could feel the slight bumps of her incipient breasts. She gripped his hands in anticipation. By the time they reached the release point, Joey could feel a swelling in his pants and was terrified that Benita might notice, but he was saved by the sudden swoop of the car as it began its descent and induced a blessed detumescence.

Without dispute, there was one ride that rose, literally, above all others for fearsomeness, and that was the Parachutes. The huge openwork steel tower, shaped like a tall mushroom, could be seen for miles. There were four arms at its top and from each arm two cables descended to the ground. Riding between these cables was a parachute, beneath which dangled a narrow seat. Two riders, or a daring single, restrained only by a leather belt, sat on this little seat. The limp parachute, from which dangled the little seat, was then hoisted to the top by another cable. The parachute was then released and there followed a terrifying moment of free fall before it billowed open and slowed the descent. Even so, the bottom was reached at a terrific speed, where large springs brought the riders to a bouncing stop. There were rumors of people spraying vomit on the crowd below, falling from the seat, and even of parachutes being blown off their cables and carrying riders away to drown in the nearby Chicago River, and indeed, the fact that the ride had to be shut down on windy days further enhanced its mystique. There were those in the neighborhood, like Joey's mother, who had never gotten up the courage to ride the Parachutes, and Joey had, in his secret heart, come to terms with the fact that he would never, even as an adult, conquer this ride. He had absolved himself of this shame by embracing his mother's dictum that you had to be crazy to ride the thing.

On this bright spring day, however, fate, in the person of Benita, would intervene. She stood there and looked up at the dizzy height of the tower, then pierced Joey with a smoldering stare and uttered those awful words, I dare you! Worse yet, she went on to say, loudly enough for everyone to hear, I will if you will!

Joey's heart sank, his stomach shriveled, his palms turned cold and wet, even his scalp tightened. Peter, Big Paulie, the other girls, even Bruno – none of whom had yet ridden the Parachutes – were staring at him. Unbelievably, Joey heard himself say jauntily, You're on! As he bought the tickets he noticed that his hand trembled, and as he and Benita waited in line his heart began to pound as loudly as the walk-through heart at the Museum of Science and Industry. Soon, Joey was outside his body watching himself, as he sometimes had in his dreams, and as they neared the loading platform he felt as if he were moving away from himself to a greater and greater distance. Not even the crushing grip of Benita's hand was enough to keep him inside his own skin. By the time the attendant strapped them into the absurdly little seat, no bigger than that of an ordinary playground swing, and buckled the flimsy restraining belts, Joey had stopped breathing and was barely alive. He looked at Benita and was surprised to see abject terror in her eyes too.

She whispered, I didn't think you would do it.

He started to shout, You're right, I won't! Let's get off! but up they started at a tremendous rate. Gripping the cables with their outside hands, the knuckles white, their inside arms wrapped around each other in a death grip, they went up so fast the blood drained from their faces. Joey tried closing his eyes, but that only increased his terror.

Benita made little whimpering sounds and gasped, I'm so scared.

Joey suppressed the momentary urge to pretend to be the brave young man, and only stammered, Me too.

The ascent seemed to last forever, long enough that despite their terror they began to be fascinated by the city spreading out below in the afternoon sun, the meandering ribbon of the Chicago River stretching to the horizon through the haze of factory smoke, the distant spires of the skyscrapers in the Loop dimly visible, and behind them the flat open expanse of Lake Michigan. My God, Joey said, it's so big. Then they stopped suddenly and dangled at the top for an eternity, not even their hearts beating. There was a sharp, metallic snap and they fell, they fell, they fell so fast their screams floated in the air above them, and at last the parachute filled with a whoosh and they slowed, swinging, floating, and they both purred with relief and pleasure at the freedom of it until they hit the springs at the bottom. As they bounced crazily to a stop, Benita turned to him and, for the second time since that day backstage, kissed him, but this time on his lips, a quick, fleeting kiss, and said, I didn't think you would do it, but I'm glad you did. They dismounted to the cheers of their subjects, and for the first time in his life, Joey took a deep breath of the rarified air at the top of the neighborhood pecking order.

By neighborhood tradition, every visit to Riverview ended with a journey through the large, gaudily painted fun house, Aladdin's Castle. It was a large building, and on its face was a huge genie with an evil smile. The front of the building was pierced here and there by walkways, and Joey and the others could watch people winding their way through the labyrinth within and listen to their screams and laughter. There was always a crowd in front of one walkway on which jets of air blew up the skirts of unwary women. Most women shuffled down the walkway clutching their skirts tightly, but a few feigned surprise and let their dresses fly up, and seemed to enjoy being the object of the crowd's hoots and catcalls. Big Paulie claimed that on his last visit he had seen a woman who had no panties on, and though Joey doubted this, he watched the procession of women with a glimmer of lascivious hope. After a time, the boys had to give in to the demands of the girls to go inside.

Depositing a nickel, each of them passed through the turnstile and climbed the ramp into the genie's leering mouth. Here Peter repeated the oft-told rumor that someone from the neighborhood had once gone in and had never come out. After a few dark tunnels, they came upon the turning barrel, through which they tried to walk and of course tripped one another until they fell in a flailing, giggling mass. Next there was the tilted room in which they pulled one another through the angled, twisting pathway, straining in the dim blue twilight like mountain climbers against the steep incline. In another passageway the floor heaved and rolled like waves, and in yet another the floorboards themselves moved forward and back randomly. Next a staircase had to be climbed as it pitched up and down like a ship in a storm. The fact that each of these contraptions could be bypassed – RIDE OR WALK, the signs said – or that bored attendants could stop the rides if needed, or that many of the passageways smelled of urine and vomit, did nothing to diminish the adventure. Soon they reached the walkway with its jets of air, and as they crossed it Joey tried to tickle Benita so she had to let go of her skirt, but she got so genuinely angry that he quickly stopped.

After the walkway they moved back inside and entered the dark maze, a series of black tunnels that had several dead ends. Around some corners there were displays that lit up when you stepped on a floorboard, one of rats in a block of cheese, and another of a peeing boy long since gone dry. At the end of the pitch-black maze there was a secret door that had to be pushed open in order to escape. Joey, Peter, Big Paulie, and Bruno ran ahead through this door, leaving the girls behind, then held it shut from the other side so that the girls couldn't find their way out. The boys giggled as they listened to the girls' growing hysteria as they thrashed around in the dark, searching for the exit. Only when the girls began to cry did Joey make the other boys relent, and the furious girls came tumbling out and chased them into the final device, a little room where you sat on a bench that flattened out and slid you down a bumpy conveyor belt that trundled you back to the outside world.

It was only when they were back in the sunshine that Joey realized Benita was crying, holding her skirt to cover the stain where she had wet herself while trapped in the dark. She looked into his eyes for a moment, a look of deep hurt and betrayal, like a kitten being thrust into a puddle. Joey was horrified, sorry, ashamed, but could find no words. She looked away and didn't speak to him again for weeks.

15 THE BLOCK PARTY

On Monday after the trip to Riverview, Joey made his usual coffee run. As he handed over the last of the bottles to Booker T, he said, We went to Riverview yesterday, you ever been?

Sure, lots of times.

What's your favorite ride?

Booker T shrugged. I dunno. I likes 'em all.

Joey puffed up his chest and said, I went on the Parachutes. He didn't add that Benita had left him no choice.

Booker T seemed unimpressed and said, Me too, lots of times.

Joey was beginning to suspect that Booker T had, in fact, never been to Riverview at all. The thought chastened him, and he wondered if Booker T knew about the Dunk the Nigger booths, and if he did, what he thought of them. A subdued Joey said only, We had a real great time.

Booker T took a sip of his chocolate milk and said, We's got something better than Riverview anyway.

Joey asked, What's that? not able to imagine anything better.

Booker T's eyes sparkled and he said, We got block parties.

What's a block party?

You don't have block parties?

I don't think so, what are they?

Oh, everybody from all around comes, the whole neighborhood. We got music and all kinds of food, really great barbecue, and it starts Saturday morning and lasts all the way to Sunday church. Fact is, we's having one next Saturday.

Joey said that his neighborhood did something like that on some of the religious holidays, even closed the street in front of Saint Michael's church and set up rides, and had a parade with a statue of the Virgin Mary.

Booker T scoffed, Ours ain't no church thing, that's for sure, excepting sometimes they's gospel singing, but mostly jazz and dancin' and drinkin' and carryin' on.

I'd sure like to see a block party.

Well, why don't you come Saturday?

Oh, I don't think my folks would let me do that.

Shit, you only do what your folks let you? What kind of pussy are you?

I could go if I wanted.

Well, then, you just take the streetcar to the El. We do it everyday.

Joey was ashamed to admit that he had never ridden the elevated train by himself and wasn't sure he could find his way. Booker T called to Luther, who came to the window and Booker T asked him, Can you write down how to get to our house for Joey?

Luther looked out at Joey in surprise, and said, What you need that for?

Booker T seemed to be enjoying Joey's growing discomfort,

and hurriedly said, Joey's gonna come to the block party Saturday, ain't you, Joey?

Joey stammered, I'm going to try.

Well, Luther said, we's just four blocks from the Sixty-third Street station. Here, I'll write it all down.

For the rest of that week, Joey carried the scrap of paper Luther had given him. He would take it out when he was alone and stare at the directions and address scrawled on it, and think about what it would be like to travel alone into the South Side. Whenever his folks or any of the other adults in the neighborhood spoke of the South Side, it was as of a foreign country, a country where *they* lived, a place driven through quickly only when necessary and then with the car doors locked, and never after dark. Joey knew that Booker T had thrown down a challenge, and increasingly felt that his dignity depended on meeting it. By Friday, he knew he would have to make a decision, and he went to ask his godfather Bruno for help.

You must be nuts, Bruno said. That's the craziest idea I ever heard, you can't go down there by yourself.

This was just the opening that Joey had hoped for, and he quickly said, How about if you come with me? Bruno resisted for a time, but Joey argued, and finally threatened that he would go by himself if necessary.

Bruno finally gave in, and admitted that he, too, had always been curious about what life on the South Side was like. He agreed that they would each tell their folks that they were spending the afternoon with the other, and would make the trip together.

They met Saturday at noon in front of the coffee shop on Western Avenue. Bruno said, It'll take almost an hour to get down there, so we can only stay about an hour, okay? When the streetcar came, Bruno asked for transfers that would carry them all the way to the South Side. The conductor lifted two transfers from his booklet and punched a series of holes in them. Joey examined his and was fascinated by the printed clock face on which the conductor had punched the time and place they had boarded.

Soon they arrived at the El station. They got off the streetcar and pushed through the iron pipe turnstiles that made a ratcheting sound like the roller coasters going uphill at Riverview. They went to the glass-enclosed booth flanked by stairs on either side. A sign said DOWNTOWN over one and DOUGLAS PARK over the other. They slid their transfers through the slot beneath the window and a huge black woman with a telephone cradled at her ear punched them in a time clock and slid them back, all without looking up or pausing in her conversation.

In the center of the small waiting room stood a potbelly stove, now cold and covered for the summer, and a row of wooden benches. On one side, a shoe shine stand with only one chair stood empty and unattended. On the other side, a small counter protruded from the wall, the dingy glass front revealing an assortment of candy bars and cigarettes. Behind the counter a wrinkled old woman in a babushka, wearing fingerless gloves even in this warmth, sorted a stack of newspapers and magazines. Almost at once, the bells rang and a bare light bulb flashed, signaling that a train was approaching. Bruno and Joey ran up the stairs marked DOWNTOWN.

The dark green car hissed and squealed and groaned as it came into the station. Joey caught a glimpse of the engineer in his tiny cab at the front of the train. The conductor was two cars behind, leaning out the top half of a window. Joey and Bruno ran to keep up with the first car as it stopped. The doors rolled open and the train sat throbbing like an impatient animal. There were only a few people inside, and Bruno managed to get the coveted first seat at the front.

Joey perched on the edge of the seat behind, the woven wicker cover stiff on the seatback that could be swiveled to face in either direction, but soon he got up and stood in the aisle next to the engineer's cab, his face pressed against the window in the front door. As they pulled out, Joey looked down and noticed the little yellow signs on the side of the platform that said 2, 4, and 6. He understood at once that they showed the engineer where to stop trains of various lengths. Above them were the signal lights that showed green over red when the way ahead was clear. The electric motors whined and they were soon zooming along at a great rate. When they rounded even a gentle curve the steel wheels screamed, and when they passed a junction in the third rail that supplied the electric power, there was a flash and a shower of sparks beneath them.

Bruno yelled, These things crash into each other sometimes if the driver falls asleep or has a heart attack. Joey glanced through a gap at the side of the dark brown window shade that covered the engineer's cab and could see a blue-black man who looked a lot like Luther holding the single handle that made the train go and stop. The man turned and saw Joey looking at him, frowned and pulled the shade closed. Joey was relieved to see that the engineer was both awake and in apparently good health.

As they slowed to approach a station, the voice of the conductor came over a speaker announcing the name of the station, but the noise of the brakes swallowed it so that Joey wasn't able to understand a thing. The train stopped at several stations, and Joey could see the tall buildings of the downtown commercial district approaching. They slowed and crossed a bridge high over the Chicago River. Up and down the river, rows of bridges full of cars crossed in many places. Bruno said, We're going into the Loop. The train headed for a narrow slot between two enormous buildings, like a cleft in a cliff face. It passed so close to the buildings that Joey could see a few people working in the offices. Soon they were on a roadbed six tracks wide that filled the entire width of the street below. Bruno said, They call this the Loop because all the overhead trains go around the whole downtown. The train slowed almost to a crawl and the wheels screeched around a tight turn. Bruno tugged at Joey's sleeve and said, We get off at the next station.

They moved to the door, clutching at the leather straps that hung from shiny pipes overhead as the car swayed and the wheels shrieked. The conductor's voice was barely audible calling, State Street, change for the subway. They had to fight their way out of the car as eager riders tried to board. Bruno led Joey across the platform and down the stairs to the street below.

The elevated tracks were supported by trussed steel pillars that cast intricate shadows on the busy street. Joey had been downtown only a few times before, most recently when his mother took him to Marshall Field's to visit Santa Claus, and they had stopped to buy fresh doughnuts made by an ingenious machine that squirted blobs of dough out of a funnel directly into hot oil, where they sizzled and floated until a wire screen conveyor rose up and carried them to the side and the attendant sprinkled them with sugar and cinnamon.

Joey and Bruno joined the throng crossing the street, past taxicabs and trucks, moving through the flashing shadows of the elevated tracks, trains rumbling above, and were carried by a flood of people into an opening in the sidewalk and down the stairs under a sign that said SOUTH SIDE. At the bottom they again showed their transfers to an attendant in a booth, who collected them. They pushed through turnstiles and moved into a dank pedestrian tunnel that smelled strongly of urine. They emerged on a platform full of people. The crowd was a mixture of whites and blacks, most of them women carrying shopping bags or with children in tow.

There was a distant rumble, then a blast of cold air. Joey leaned out as far as he dared and peered past the dirty white tiles into the gaping maw of the tunnel. A dim headlamp of a train was approaching, and by its light Joey could see the black walls of the tunnel and a trickle of water between the ties on the roadbed. With a sudden roar, the train burst from the mouth of the tunnel, wheels squealing, a red letter R in its window. They boarded the middle car where the conductor was leaning out the window. The car was full, and Joey and Bruno stood close together, clutching one of the shiny pipes that ran from floor to ceiling near the doors. The conductor had to try several times to close the doors, and the train finally pulled out.

The people stood impassive in utter silence as the train swayed and rumbled on. Out the window, Joey could see a maze of cables and pipes that ran along the walls of the tunnel and signal lights flashed by so quickly he wondered how they would stop in time if one suddenly changed to red. He began reading the advertisements on long placards on the curved ceiling of the car, ads for shorthand training, cigarettes, and hemorrhoid medicines. Another station flashed by but the train didn't stop. Joey could see people packed tightly on the platform, standing precariously close to the edge. He looked up at Bruno who, as if reading his mind, leaned close and said over the noise, Sometimes people fall in front of the train by accident, or sometimes they commit suicide that way, or get murdered when somebody pushes them.

Soon the train began climbing and emerged into the daylight. They stopped at a series of stations and at each a number of people got off, though almost no one got on. As the car gradually emptied, Joey noticed that most of the people getting off were white, and that the population of the car was becoming steadily more and more black. When they reached Fifty-third Street, the last of the white passengers left. Joey and Bruno were now the only white people in the car and were feeling out of place, but no one seemed to pay any attention. As they approached Sixty-third Street, Bruno nodded to Joey. This is where Luther's instructions told them to get off.

They took the stairs down from the station into a very different world. The trusses of the elevated tracks were the same, but the street below had an entirely different rhythm than the hustle-bustle of State Street. Here people lounged on the steps of storefronts and on chairs, talking, laughing, and smoking. At the curb, several carts were selling ices and watermelon, and on each block at least one barbeque stand filled the air with deliciously pungent smoke. They walked across a wide street named Cottage Grove Avenue. The sound of music drifted out of a club over which a large sign proclaimed MCKEE FITZHUGH'S DISC JOCKEY LOUNGE.

Still following Booker T's directions, they walked two streets down and turned right onto a residential street named Drexel Avenue. The houses on Drexel Avenue were large, but very old and in disrepair. Here too, people sat on their colonnaded porches and stoops, sipping tea from mason jars or swigging bottles of beer or wine. Some of them fell silent as Joey and Bruno walked by, staring with surprise, some with amusement. One boy called out, You two lost? and several people laughed.

Joey smiled and answered, Just visiting a friend, he told me there was a party today.

The boy's mother raised a fleshy arm and pointed down the block, calling, Right straight ahead, you can't miss it.

Joey called, Thanks, and waved, and the boy and his mother waved back.

As they moved away, Bruno muttered quietly, We must be crazy.

Sure enough, two blocks ahead they could see, hear, and smell the block party. A haze of barbecue smoke rose from several charcoal burners made from large metal drums cut in half. As they neared, they heard jazz coming from one of the houses near the middle of the block where a dancing, clapping crowd spilled onto the sidewalk. That's it, Bruno said, glancing at Luther's instructions. People were still gathering from blocks around, and Joey and Bruno moved through the growing crowd, virtually unnoticed.

As they approached the house, Booker T appeared on the front steps and saw Joey below. He rushed down, smiling and eyes wide, saying, Damn! I never thought you'd really come! I was just calling your bluff!

Joey introduced Bruno, and Booker T said they should come inside. We got some mean jazz going on. We got the Hawk himself in here!

As they threaded their way up the stairs through the crowd, Joey asked, Who's the Hawk?

Booker T looked back and laughed, Shit, you never heard of Coleman Hawkins? He's playing over to the Winter Garden and he come by to play with some old friends.

Inside, the crowd was solid, wall to wall, various shades of black skin glistening with sweat, throbbing in perfect unison to the breathtakingly fast tempo of drums, a bass fiddle, and an upright piano at which a pianist, his shirt soaked through, pounded. Bruno held back at the doorway, but Joey followed Booker T into the middle of the crowd. Leaning against the piano, squeezed next to the bass fiddle, was a slender man wearing dark glasses and a porkpie hat made of straw, playing a golden tenor saxophone from which poured an unbroken and endless stream of notes, melodic phrases that rose and fell like a bird in flight and caught Joey and lifted him, carrying him wherever they went, filled with emotions he had experienced only in his dreams. At one moment the sax cried with despair, the next it laughed uproariously, then suddenly turned seductive and the women in the room moaned with pleasure and the men purred in sympathy. Like everyone else in the room, Joey soon had sweat streaming down his face, soaking his shirt, but he had lost all sense of his separate physical body; he was part of the pulsating organism that filled the room, moving in perfect synchronization and responding to the slightest nuance of the music. Booker T was beside him, smiling, and leaned close and said into his ear, You ever be a colored man on a Saturday night, you never want to be a white man again.

When at last the music ended and the shouting and applause died down as the musicians broke for a smoke, whiskey, and barbeque, Joey waved Bruno in from the doorway as Booker T led them into the kitchen. There were only a few people in the kitchen, all watching quietly and intently a man sitting in the middle of the room with a bedsheet tucked into his collar. Behind the man stood Luther brandishing a pearl-handled straight razor. Joey and Bruno exchanged a glance and for a moment Joey remembered the talk of neighborhood boys about black men and razors, but they soon saw that in his other hand Luther had a comb, and with razor and comb was carefully cutting the man's hair. There was a half-empty bottle of Old Overholt whiskey on the table and every so often, Luther would pause between cuts and take a healthy swig. Booker T whispered to Joey, Uncle Luther gives the best razor cuts on the South Side. When Luther declared the man finished and brushed him off, Booker T said, Look here, Uncle Luther, look who come to the party.

Luther smiled in amazement when he saw Joey, saying, Coffee boy! I'll be damned! You really come down here all by yourself?

Joey gestured to Bruno and said, My godfather here helped me come.

Luther smiled, closed the razor, and extended his hand. Bruno took it and they shook, Luther saying, Ain't that something! Good for you!

Bruno said, Pleased to meet you, sir, Joey has told me a lot about you.

Luther smiled and said, Well, it's only half true, and that's the good part. He glanced down at Joey's hair and said, You look like you could use some cuttin'. How about it?

Joey tried to beg off, saying he didn't have any money, but Luther scoffed and said he never charged on party days and wouldn't take no for an answer. Soon Joey was in the chair, the bedsheet around his neck, and Luther was working his magic on both Joey's hair and the whiskey bottle. Joey held perfectly still and stared at Bruno, his mouth smiling but his eyes frightened. Bruno stared back, his face alight with amusement.

An eternity later, the bottle nearly empty, Luther brushed the cuttings off Joey and whisked aside the bedsheet. He held out a mirror for Joey to see his fine haircut, which was indeed a thing of beauty. Joey was so relieved and happy that he nearly cried, pumping Luther's hand and repeating that it was the best haircut he had ever had, that Luther would be getting free coffee all week.

Luther looked down at Joey and laughed. Then he grew serious and said quietly, Look, I know this wasn't easy for you boys, but we're glad you came. You see, coffee boy, it don't matter what's on the outside of us. He reached over and tapped Joey's head. What counts is what's up here. Then he tapped Joey's chest. And most of all, what's in here.

On the way back home, Joey and Bruno sat in the swaying

El car and ate the barbequed chicken that Luther had insisted they take with them. Joey watched the backs of the houses as they flashed past, most of them with wooden porches stacked up like playing cards, festooned with laundry hanging from lines and potted tomato plants. He imagined what it was like for Luther and Booker T to take this hour-long trip twice every working day. He remembered Luther's words and touch. And most of all he listened in his mind to the echoes of the Hawk's saxophone, remembering how it had felt to be so transported, so part of that crowded room, so completely absorbed and yet free. He knew then that he could no longer avoid the question that had been forming in his mind ever since the day that Luther first asked him to go for coffee, and Bruno was the only one he could ask.

Bruno, Joey said, leaning close so Bruno could hear him over the sound of the train, can I ask you something important?

Sure, Bruno said, what is it?

Joey searched for the right words, then said straight out, Why does everybody hate Negroes so much?

Bruno raised his eyebrows and looked around to see if any of the other riders, all of them black, were listening. But Joey couldn't stop, the words poured out. I mean, he said, the way everybody talks about them. And the way they seem to have the worst jobs, and the way Booker T has to work instead of going to school, and those awful booths at Riverview, the way they have to live only here on the South Side, and the way we always lock our car doors when we drive through here. I mean, you and me, we had a good time at the block party. Everybody treated us real good. And I think that if things were different, Booker T could be as good a friend to me as any of the kids, and a lot better than Rex or some of the others. Why should it make so much difference that his skin is darker than mine? When

I hear somebody say nigger like that, even my father, I want to say, that's wrong, you shouldn't say that or treat them like that. Why is it like that?

Joey was spent and fell silent, expectant. Bruno was quiet for a time. Finally he said, That's a good question, Joey. I've wondered about it myself. I don't know why it is. I guess some of it is just because they're different, and people are afraid of people that are different than they are. The bad jobs, and the bad schools, that goes all the way back to slavery. As far as living on the South Side, I think maybe people like to stick together, just like there are Italian neighborhoods and Irish neighborhoods, and Polish. Chicago is just that kind of a city. But the rest, the fear, the disgust… I don't know. Negroes fought in the War just like everybody else. But most white people, even the people in our families, don't seem to count that. They aren't bad people, but they have some wrong ideas and some wrong feelings. Maybe that will change some day.

Joey said, It should, it should change.

Bruno put his hand on Joey's shoulder and said, I guess the main thing is how you feel inside, and how you decide to act for yourself. That's where it has to start.

That's what Luther said too. It's what's in our heart that matters. But I don't know, it's scary to act different than everybody else.

Yes, it's real scary. But I think God doesn't want us to be the way we are sometimes.

God? Joey asked. He sat back. He had never thought about God being concerned with the way people think or feel or act. But if that were true, another question had to be asked. Bruno, Joey said, if God doesn't want things to be the way they are, why doesn't he just change them?

Bruno smiled and said, That's our job, Joey. Then Bruno got

very quiet. After a time, he said, I'll tell you a secret I haven't told anybody. Promise not to say anything?

Joey nodded and made the Sign of the Cross and said, Cross my heart and hope to die.

Well, Bruno said, I'm going to be a priest. I've thought about it a lot, and I think I have to do it. I'm going into the seminary as soon as I finish high school.

Wow, Joey said. Wow. He looked at Bruno, pudgy Bruno with his thick glasses that made his eyes seem huge, and tried to imagine him in the black suit with the white collar, and calling him Father Bruno. To Joey's surprise, it felt perfectly right. It was easy to think of Bruno as a priest. Joey smiled at Bruno and said, You're going to be a great priest. Lots better than Father Louis, for sure.

Bruno laughed, and his laughter changed their mood. The time for philosophy was over. He reached into the bag for a piece of chicken, then looked up at Joey's head and said, So, what are you going to tell your parents?

Joey shook the image of Father Bruno from his mind and said, I thought we were going to say we were at each other's houses.

Sure, Bruno said, but what about the haircut?

Oh Lord, joey said. He thought frantically for a time, but nothing came. I'll keep my hat on, he said at last, maybe they won't notice. Bruno laughed so hard he almost choked on the chicken.

During the rest of the trip, Joey formed a plan to explain the haircut. As soon as he and Bruno got back to the neighborhood, Joey dipped into his coffee money and went to see Silvio, the barber, and insisted on paying for a trim. Silvio dutifully put him in the chair and clipped a little with his scissors, but aside from shortening Joey's sideburns, he could find nothing to do. Finally, he said, This is the best haircut I've ever seen. Where'd you get it?

A friend, Joey said.

Well, Silvio said, I hope it's nobody around here or he'll put me out of business.

No, Joey said, he lives far away. Very far away.

16 QUEEN OF HEAVEN

IT WAS A FEW WEEKS AFTER THE BLOCK PARTY, and Joey was enjoying one of their Sunday afternoon visits to his mother's folks, Nonna Severina and Nonno Lorenzo, who lived in a new brick house in the suburb of North Riverside. As the grown-ups talked, smoked, and had coffee and *biscotti* upstairs, Joey was on his own, exploring in the basement.

He played for a time with the old slot machine, now activated by metal washers instead of nickels, that his grandfather had gotten from a crony who worked at one of the Mafia clubs in nearby Cicero. There being little thrill in winning a handful of washers, Joey soon grew tired of the slot machine and began to poke into drawers and shelves. He noticed a long cardboard tube atop one of the bookcases. He got on a chair and took it down. From it he withdrew a roll of heavy fabric. Excited, he unrolled it and revealed an elaborate coat of arms. His mother had told him with great pride that his Nonno Lorenzo had been an embroiderer in Italy, and had shown him medals that Nonno had won from the Palace of Fine Arts in Florence. Joey knew at once that this coat of arms, unfinished at the bottom, was his grandfather's work, and was probably the coat of arms of his mother's family, the Chiostris. He examined the intricate stitching with real wonder, imagining his grandfather's fingers wielding the needle. Mother had explained that Nonno Lorenzo had tried to pursue his profession in America, but there was no call for embroiderers here, so Nonno reluctantly had gone to work filing gear-teeth by hand for International Harvester. Joey held the tapestry, imagining it hanging in the Chiostri villa which, according to family lore, still stood in a little village near Pescia and was so grand it had a theatre on the third floor, and four tenant farms attached.

Suddenly there was a great cry from upstairs and the sound of running feet. Joey hurriedly put the cloth back in its tube and ran up the stairs. He was met in the kitchen by his mother, pale and breathless, who told him, Something's happened to Nonno, stay here till I call you. After more running and shouting, Joey heard a siren in the distance. He peered out from the kitchen door into the living room, shivering as the siren grew nearer. He could barely breathe when it stopped in front of the house, its wail dropping into a throaty purr and finally dying away as the firemen rushed through the front door carrying a large suitcase on which the letters PULMOTOR were stenciled. Mother called to the firemen, and they ran upstairs, the flashing red light pouring in behind them.

Joey could hear hushed voices upstairs and the cries of his grandmother, *Dio Caro, Dio Caro, non gli permetta morire, cosa farò,* Oh God, don't let him die, what will I do? and the comforting voices of his mother and father, *Loro si prenderanno cura di lui, sta bene*, they'll take care of him, it'll be fine. Sick with fear, Joey stood in the kitchen, holding back tears and thinking desperately of something he could do to help. Then he remembered the miracle wrought by BisNonno Pucci when Great-Aunt Delia had stopped breathing. Joey ran to the refrigerator and got an egg, took a cereal bowl from the cabinet and a fork from a drawer. He went to the base of the stairs, just inside the front door, and stood there with his egg, cereal bowl, and fork. His mother came down and saw him, saying, What are you doing out here, Joey, go back in the kitchen. He held out the egg, bowl and fork, and said, Here, do like BisNonno Pucci did for Aunt Delia. Mother looked at the egg, bowl, and fork a moment, then, as recognition dawned, broke into tears and hugged Joey tight.

Another siren approached and died, and an ambulance pulled in behind the fire truck. Joey's father rushed downstairs to the door and yelled to the attendants, Upstairs in the bedroom. He glanced gravely at Mother and Joey, shaking his head. The attendants came in with a stretcher, and Father led them upstairs. For a long time, Joey and his mother stood there in the living room holding each other until Mother buried Joey's head in her bosom as the attendants carried Nonno Lorenzo down the stairs, covered with a white sheet and strapped to the stretcher. Joey peered out from his mother's embrace and could see his grandfather, gaunt and pale, unshaven as always, so tall that his feet dangled off the end of the stretcher, for he was called *Lungo*, the long one. His usually bright eyes were vacant, and his open mouth gaped like a fish's under the plastic mask of the pulmotor. They rushed him out to the ambulance as Nonna Severina, wailing uncontrollably, was helped down the stairs by his father. As they passed, his father said, We'll go to the hospital, you stay here, the others will be coming, we'll call and let you know. The ambulance pulled away, its siren rising. The fire truck rumbled to life and followed.

Soon Aunt Mary and Uncle Louis, who lived nearby, arrived, saying that others were on the way. It was agreed that too many visitors at the hospital would only complicate things, so only Uncle Louis would join Father and Nonna there. In the hour that followed, the phone rang often and the news was repeated to one caller after another. The family telephone network was activated, each person knowing without being told whom they should call in turn. More and more people began to arrive, some of them relatives whom Joey had seen before only at weddings and funerals. They gathered in the living room, in the dining room, in the kitchen, spilled over to the stoop, and finally the sidewalk. Some smoked, some paced silently, some prayed, some murmured words of hope. Joey's mother made coffee and Aunt Mary rushed to her nearby home to get cakes, cookies, and pastries.

Finally a call came from the hospital. Joey's mother took it in the kitchen, listened silently, then came into the living room, looking grave. She said simply, They've sent for the priest. In unison, everyone made a quiet, sad sound. They all knew the priest was not called lightly.

Soon, another call came. Mother came out again and had to steady herself in the doorway. She didn't need to speak, but she did. He's gone, she said.

Joey looked at his mother, leaning with one hand against the wall. He went to her and took her other hand, but she seemed not to notice. He tried to comprehend this thing she had said. He had thought about death, but this was not like anything he had imagined. This was not anything. It was an absence, quiet and empty and still and unfathomable. He stood there unable to do anything but hold his mother's hand. Then Mother reached down and embraced him with both arms, so tightly he couldn't breathe for a moment, and he felt her body shake. Then there were people pressed around them, holding them, wailing, rocking.

Eventually his mother quieted and people led her to the sofa. There were words of comfort, remembrances of Lorenzo stretching back to the old country, anecdotes of courageous acts, wry stories. Finally some of the other women served a late supper, some broth, ravioli, chicken, salad, and pastries, just a little bite to keep spirits up. His mother helped to clean up.

A few days later, the family accompanied Nonna Severina for the first viewing of the body. They passed in silence through the familiar doors of Anzilotti's Funeral Home, which until that day had been for Joey merely one of many buildings on Oakley Avenue, distinguished only by its castle-like carved stone façade. Inside, they were met by Leo Anzilotti himself, a friendly, short man who was normally as gregarious and as easy-going as any of the older men who gathered across the street at the Po Piedmont Club to play *briscola* or *bocce* or simply to sit and smoke cigars and tell old tales. But today he was in a plain dark suit and stood so erect, with quiet dignity, that he seemed taller. He murmured his sorrow and showed them the guest book, prayer cards, and flowers that had been carefully arranged inside the main viewing room.

Joey and his mother hung back as his father and Leo took Nonna forward toward the casket, which sat on a brass stand with a purple velvet cover surrounded by flowers. Leo raised the satin-lined lid of the casket. His mother squeezed Joey, and he was grateful that he couldn't see the body inside. Nonna looked down, then cried out and staggered. Father and Leo held her up and helped her out into the hall where she was lowered, crying, onto a chair. Mother took Father aside and whispered, What's wrong?

Father whispered back, His hair is parted on the wrong side.

Joey and his mother comforted Nonna while inside Joey could see his father and Leo busily bent over the casket. Soon they returned and father said, There, it's all right now, just fine, come and see.

Leo said, I'm so sorry, the girl didn't know him, he had his hat on in the picture, I should have seen to it myself, we did our best.

And of course Leo was forgiven, and Nonna said that Nonno now looked just fine, better than he had in life.

The three days that followed passed as if in a dream, most of them spent sitting on a folding chair in the viewing room, the air growing heavier with the sickly sweet smell of ripening flowers, an odor that would forever after awaken in Joey a fear of death. The immediate family sat in the front rows, and hour after hour, people came to gaze at the body and offer comfort to the bereaved. Relatives Joey had never met were there, and a great stir accompanied the arrival of Great-Uncle Cesare, who had flown all the way from Bakersfield, California. Joey had heard stories about his great-uncles, the brothers Cesare and Napolean, Nappy for short, who had together made a great fortune in the twenties as civil engineers, designing many of the bridges in Chicago. Like their namesakes, Cesare and Nappy had dreams of grandeur. In 1935 they took all the money they had made in Chicago and went back to Italy, intending to restore the family villa and live like country gentlemen. Mother's side of the family prided itself on being descended from nobility, a great-great-uncle having been a *cavaliere*, which Mother said was something like a duke, under the last king. The family's land included four *poderes*, tenant farms, on which flowers were grown, that being the family's traditional business. Cesare and Nappy bought the villa and began its restoration. They had poor timing, however, and in 1936, Mussolini nationalized the family's land without compensation. Cesare wisely retreated to America, but Napolean vowed to fight on. He stayed, taking an apartment in the family's ancestral seat, Col di Buggiano, a medieval Tuscan hill town enclosed by broad stone walls. Nappy railed against Mussolini and his Brown Shirts so fiercely that one day the local *fascisti* took him up on the broad town walls, tied his pant bottoms with twine, forced him to drink mineral oil, and made him walk around and around the town in his own excrement, beating him whenever he fell. He died the next day, and the family fortune was seized to help make the trains run on time.

On the third night of the wake, Father Louis came. Bruno came with him, dressed in his altar boy regalia and carrying a smoking censer that filled the room with the heavy aroma of incense. He and Father Louis knelt in front of the casket and led the mourners in a Novena. Rosary beads slipped slowly one by one through the fingers of the faithful, while Joey wriggled on the hard folding chair. Benita was there with her folks, and she caught his eye with a glance toward the door. She turned to her mother and whispered something, then went out. Joey took his cue and whispered to his mother that he had to go the bathroom. He slipped out through the heavy velvet curtains and found Benita waiting for him in the dark hallway. She said, I'm sorry about your Nonno, mine died last year and it was sad.

Joey said, Yeah, it is.

Benita looked at the dark velvet-covered walls and said, It's spooky in here.

Joey brightened and said, Do you want to look around?

Benita was excited at the idea but said, I can't stay away real long, I said I was just going to the bathroom.

The two of them tiptoed down the hall toward the rear of the building. They passed two other empty viewing rooms and went through a curtain. Joey pushed open the door of a storeroom that was filled with brass flower stands, the little benches that you kneel on to pray, casket supports, and other heavy, shiny implements of mortuary display. At the end of the hall was a door with a sign,

EMPLOYEES ONLY, and Joey and Benita looked at each other. Benita said again, Go ahead, I dare you. Joey pushed the door open. The smell of formaldehyde washed over them as they stepped inside a cool, plain room with shiny white walls. In the center, dim under a single fluorescent light, was a body-sized stainless steel table with a gutter all the way around its edge and a drain at one end, beneath which sat a large, shiny bucket. Hanging above the table was the sort of adjustable light one sees in operating rooms, and next to it, dangling from a hook at the end of a long hose coming from a large machine, was a spear-like probe. It took only a glance for both of them to understand that this was the instrument through which the viscera were sucked, and they bumped into one another in their rush to get out the door.

Back in the hallway, Joey's mother was just coming out of the viewing room. There you are, she said in a whisper, where were you two? Come on, it's time to say goodbye to Nonno. Joey looked at Benita, who squeezed his hand. He followed his mother back into the viewing room. For the past three days, Joey had assiduously avoided looking at his grandfather's body, but now he knew he could avoid it no longer. Everyone murmured sympathetically at the sight of the only grandson approaching the bier, but Joey was more than anything curious about seeing his first dead body. He was surprised that Nonno looked much as he had in life, though the waxy make-up made him look like a statue of himself, and Joey could not help thinking that this was only a hollow effigy of his Nonno, that everything inside had been sucked out by the cruel metal probe hanging in the back room. His mother whispered, Kiss him goodbye. Joey swallowed and bent forward. Nonno's cheek was cold and dry, and smelled like the embalming room.

Joey stepped back and the rest of the family came forward,

Nonna Severina needing to be held, as Leo Anzilotti closed the lid of the satin-lined casket. Leo looked down at Joey, his eyes soft and filled with sympathy. Joey wondered if it was Leo himself who wielded the metal probe, and was awestruck by the realization that this unassuming man possessed the deepest secrets of mortality and knew the ultimate truth about everyone in this room more completely than their parents or loved ones, and yet could regard them all with such quiet affection. Joey thought, What a strange thing life is, and death even stranger. Bruno was standing off to one side with his censer, watching Joey closely. Joey looked at him and saw understanding in his eyes.

The next day, in the church of St. Michael the Archangel, the coffin stood in the center aisle, atop it a picture of Nonno. After the Solemn High Mass, Joey watched the procession as the coffin was carried by his father, his Uncle Louis, Silvio the barber, Benita's father Fan, Leo Anzilotti himself, and Matseo the nine-fingered carpenter, who had stuffed himself into his World War I uniform for the occasion. Behind the casket tottered BisNonno Pucci, hatless and pipeless for once, arm-in-arm with Nonna Severina, both of them assisted by Joey's mother and Aunts Mary and Diana, and after them shuffled the entire parish. On the street, Leo Anzilotti personally guided the casket as it was placed on a platform and swung into the hearse by a silent mechanism that fascinated Joey. The flowers were loaded into the open-backed flower car as everyone got into their automobiles, funeral placards in the windows. The immediate family rode in a limousine behind the hearse and the flower car. With one police motorcycle at the head and another behind, the whole procession pulled away from the church. Lights on, they drove slowly through the neighborhood. People lined the street, men doffed their hats, women in babushkas made the Sign of the Cross.

Once outside the neighborhood they drove faster, beyond the

city and into the suburbs, then slowly past Nonno's house in North Riverside. They turned north for a time and at last pulled into Queen of Heaven Cemetery, past the rows of gravestones on the landscaped grounds, and stopped in front of the huge stone mausoleum. The mourners gathered as the coffin was placed on a trolley and rolled inside. Everyone followed, and the murmur of prayer echoed against the marble walls as Father Louis led them over and over in the Our Father, the Hail Mary, and the Prayer for the Dead. High up one of the marble walls, a slab had been removed to reveal a gaping black hole the size of the casket. The slab itself rested against the wall on the floor, waiting to be replaced, Nonno's name and dates already engraved on its face. The dim light coming through the stained glass windows cast a blue pall on the crowd as the casket came to a stop at the base of the wall beneath the opening. The priest's voice rose, intoning in Latin, there was a whir, and the casket began miraculously to rise, lifted by a chromed scissors jack hidden inside the trolley. Up and up it rose, ten, twenty feet in the air, and when it was at the level of the hole in the wall, there was another whir and the casket began to slide slowly into oblivion.

At this moment Joey realized that lurking just behind that entire expanse of marble, divided into hundreds of small graven squares, was a whole city of the dead. As if with X-ray vision, he saw the multitude of coffins stacked like cereal boxes at the A&P, and in each the decomposing remains of untold grandfathers and grandmothers. The sheer barbarity of it exploded in his mind. More than the sight of the embalming room, more than the chemical smell of his dead grandfather, more than the touch of the cold, dry cheek on his lips, the sight of that casket disappearing slowly, inexorably, into the marble wall, soon to be sealed, filled Joey with his first real dread, and was replayed in his dreams for years.

17 IN THE STREET

As the fullness of summer approached and the warm weather finally held, the life of the neighborhood, and especially of the children, moved into the street. On this block that was Joey's world no door was ever locked. Children called to one another by standing on the sidewalk in front of the house and yelling, Yo-oooh Paulie, whereupon Paulie would come out to play, or an adult would appear at a window and call, Paulie can't come out, he's sick, or he's being punished for stealing. Most of the families on the street, having come from the same villages in Tuscany, were related in some way, so that the neighborhood was in fact one large extended family. The most intimate details were freely shared, and bedwetters were quickly cured by the soiled sheets being hung out on public view to dry. Children would often enter a house without knocking, asking, is Guido home, or, Can I use your bathroom? When a child was in trouble, help was as close as the nearest adult. Conversely, when a child was seen misbehaving, any adult in the neighborhood had the full authority of a parent, and a slap or a spank could be visited on the wrongdoer from any direction. As a result, the children were free to allow their hostilities to flare into violence, knowing that an adult, or the older kids, would restrain them before any damage worse than a bloody nose or bruised eye could be inflicted.

This, however, was not a fortunate situation for Joey. He was a few years older than the little kids on the block, and several years younger than the older kids, so he had to choose between the humiliation of playing with the little kids, or getting the shit kicked out of him playing with the older kids. Pride aside, Joey enjoyed playing with the little kids, mainly because Benita, who was the only other kid on the block his age, also played with them. They played classic games like Ring Around the Rosy, Hopscotch, Simon Says, and Follow the Leader. They also played marbles, which Joey usually won. He kept his large collection in a red Hills Brothers coffee can, and was especially fond of his cat's eyes, though the best marble of all was his huge green bowler that had specks of blue and red inside. He would often hold it to the light and let his gaze wander in it like a tiny universe.

But pride dictated that Joey played most of the time with the older boys, who found endless ways of tormenting him. Rex had discovered that ever since his Nonno had died, Joey had an uncontrollable fear of emergency vehicles, and whenever an ambulance or fire truck went through the neighborhood, siren wailing, Rex or one of his cronies would tell Joey that the pulmotor squad had come for his mother, whereupon Joey would invariably run home in terror while they laughed at his gullibility. For the rest of his life the sound of a siren made his blood run cold.

Joey's troubles with the older boys came to a head one Saturday morning when he foolishly took his favorite stuffed bear, Mr. Teddy, outside with him. Seeing him with it, Rex sneered, Lookit the little boy with his dollie. Joey started to retreat toward his house, but Rex grabbed Mr. Teddy and tossed it to Primo. Joey ran after it, but Primo tossed Teddy over his head to Secundo. This game of keep-away continued as Joey ran from one to the other in growing desperation. Finally, Rex kicked Mr. Teddy like a football and he came apart. Joey was grief-stricken and ran home clutching the precious pieces. When he tearfully explained what had happened, his father became enraged that Joey had failed to stand up to the older kids, and insisted that he go back out and confront them. When Joey refused, his father dragged him by the arm down the gangway, shouting, Stand up! Stand up! while Joey shrieked in terror. On the street, an ugly scene ensued between Joey's father and the older boys. Joey shrank in mortification, sure that he would be a pariah forevermore, having violated the cardinal rule against involving parents in a kid dispute. The argument brought people out onto their front stoops, and Bruno came running from his house across the street. Seeing Joey's pain, Bruno, though himself one of the older boys, sidled next to Joey and whispered, Don't worry, it doesn't matter what these guys think, I'll take care of you from now on. And from then on, he did.

Once he was under the protection of the future Father Bruno, Joey began to actually enjoy playing with the older boys. They sometimes went on quests into the surrounding neighborhoods, their favorite to the streetcar barns on Twenty-sixth Street and Leavitt, about six blocks away. On Saturdays during the lunch hour, when few workmen were around, they would creep up the street toward the car barn under cover of parked cars. Joey was fascinated by the rows of glistening green cars, the maze of tracks imbedded years ago in the brick streets, the turntable that directed the cars onto one track or another when they entered or left the barn, and the powerful smell of ozone from the sparks made by the trolleys as they passed over the junctions in the web of electrical lines overhead. The boys were drawn to the car barns by the cylindrical canvas bags that hung on hooks at the doors of each track. These bags were full of the cancelled transfers that the conductors collected on each run, transfers that were exactly the size and shape of paper money and were used in the various games of chance the boys played, card games like *Briscola* or *Sette Bella*. The transfers had a real value derived from the danger involved in stealing them from the bags, a maneuver that required a stealthy approach across the maze of tracks, a quick grab into a bag, and a hasty retreat as the streetcar workers invariably chased them.

On one of these sorties, Rex decided on a multiple attack, each boy taking a different row of streetcars. They can't chase all of us, he said with the impeccable logic of a twelve-year-old. He decided which boy would take which track, assigning Joey to the furthest, most exposed track, a target which required crossing all the other tracks as they spread through the switches, branching lane after lane like the root system of a steel tree. Bruno began to complain on Joey's behalf, but Joey silenced him with a look which said, in effect, It's okay, I can handle it. On Rex's signal, the boys burst from their hiding place behind a parked car and sprinted to their assigned tracks.

His heart pounding, Joey reached the end doorway and dug his hands into the bulging canvas bag. He pulled out a double handful of transfers and was escaping undetected when he caught his foot in one of the switches imbedded in the pavement. He fell heavily and felt a pop in his ankle. The transfers went flying in a great flurry of paper. At first, the shock of falling was so great he didn't feel anything, but seconds later he felt a terrible pain in his ankle. He wanted to yell, but pride held him back. He tried to get up, but for some reason his right leg wouldn't work. He lay there helpless in a pool of transfers while the other boys made their escape, laughing.

His tears blurred his vision, but he could just make out the great green streetcar on his track moving. It was lurching out of the barn and straight at him, traveling backward. Through the rear window Joey could see the trainman at the front, talking animatedly to someone unseen in the car ahead, oblivious of the boy lying helpless in his path. Joey began to shout, but the rumbling of the car and the sizzle of the sparking overhead wires drowned him out. Nearer and nearer it came, swaying a little as it moved. Joey started to drag himself off the tracks, but a wave of nausea and searing pain swept him. He felt himself growing light, as if he were rising into the air, his vision darkened, and everything began to swim. It felt, he thought, just like when the Riverview parachute drops and you float for a while, only not as scary. Then it was all dark and silent.

A voice came into the darkness from far away. Joey, Joey, it called. A luminous fog formed and gradually the voice got louder and the figure of Bruno emerged. He was looking down at Joey, holding him under the arms. They were on the sidewalk next to the car barns.

Another voice said, Is he okay, wow, that was close, and Peter's face peered down beside Bruno's.

Joey felt strangely serene. He looked up and said, Hi, guys, what's going on?

Bruno said, You almost got run over, that's what.

Yeah, that streetcar would've sliced you in two, Bruno pulled you out just in time, Peter said.

Joey looked up at Bruno, who nodded grimly. Yup, he said, you almost bought it.

Oh, Joey said, oh.

Then it was dark and silent again.

The thick bandage was on Joey's ankle for two weeks. His parents knew only that he had tripped on the streetcar tracks, and had been spared the details, although Joey longed to tell them of Bruno's heroism. He was able to hobble around on a crutch, and enjoyed the ribbing from the other kids who called him Billy Batson, the crippled newsboy who could turn into Captain Marvel. He continued to go to school, and even managed to haul the coffee basket with his free hand. The lady in the coffee shop was especially solicitous and gave him an extra jelly doughnut each morning.

His ankle prevented Joey from joining one of the most cherished rituals of early summer. On the hottest days, Joey's dad would take his biggest pipe wrench from the furnace room and open the hydrant in front of their house so that a great plume of water shot out into the street. The kids would run through the plume, sliding on the wet pavement, splashing one another. Cars and trucks slowed as they went through, and eventually a fire truck would arrive and everyone would vanish into the houses as the long-suffering firemen closed the hydrant. A few years later, this summer ritual would end as polio swept the country, the streets emptied, and everyone with kids huddled in their sweltering houses praying to the Virgin Mary and Sister Kenney.

18 THE DAIRY MAID

Two weeks after his bandage was removed, school closed for summer vacation. On the last day of school, Joey made his last coffee run. As he passed the bottles through the window to Booker T, he said, I'm going away for the summer and I won't be bringing coffee until I get back. Maybe you can get the coffee until I get back in the fall.

Booker T looked out and asked, Where you goin'?

Joey said, We're going to Michigan for the summer, we been going every summer, long as I can remember.

Booker T grunted, Shit, ain't that nice. I'd sure like to go to Michigan, play on the beach. But yeah, maybe I can get the coffee.

Joey immediately regretted what sounded like bragging and went on, But it's not so great, it's just an old farmhouse where we stay.

Booker T grunted again, I bet it beats this shit hole.

Joey was really uncomfortable now. He put the wire basket down next to the window. Here, he said, you can use the basket, come and get it after work. Booker T gathered up the bottles without comment and disappeared inside. Well, Joey called to the empty window, see ya. And thanks for inviting me to the block party. There was no answer and Joey backed away, not knowing what else to say or do, and went home to pack.

For as long as Joey could remember, his family had spent the summer in a small, rural community called Stevensville, Michigan, near the city of St. Joseph, which they all called simply St. Joe. It was only some thirty miles away straight across Lake Michigan, but an arduous ninety-mile drive around the bottom of the lake on a motley collection of highways and city streets. This year, the trip was special for two reasons. First, Father had been promoted to general foreman, and because of his extra pay, Mother was able to quit her job and devote full time to raising Joey as a good American. Second, after years of scrimping, his parents had saved enough to buy a new car and retire the venerable Packard, which had for years been patched together by Father with parts picked during frequent trips to the junkyards of Cicero. The new car was a Hudson, a squat behemoth that his father proudly asserted was built like a tank and weighed over 4000 pounds. It was advertised by a Chicago sports announcer aptly named Jack Brickhouse, who said the Hudson had many of the qualities of the great Chicago Bears running back, Bronco Nagurski, who had once carried most of an opposing team into the end zone on his back and was stopped only when he ran into the goal post head on. When they revived him, he said he was all right, but they should sign up that last guy who hit him.

Joey thought that the Hudson had a bovine quality, and named it Bedelia. Though beloved by the men of the family, Bedelia was not a favorite of the women. When Italian families went driving, the women always rode in the back, and since they always wore hats, the overhead clearance in the back seat was a prime consideration in the choice of a car. Bedelia, low and streamlined, was woefully inadequate in this regard, but father argued that it compensated by being safe. You could get hit by a truck, he said proudly, and it would barely dent the thing.

His Nonno Beppino and Nonna Augusta had gone to spend the summer visiting relatives in Italy, a trip they had promised themselves for years. But his other grandmother, Nonna Severina, would be with them on the trip to Stevensville, spending her first summer alone since the death of Nonno Lorenzo.

It was traditional for a number of families to travel together in a caravan for the three-hour drive. Father insisted they get an early start to beat the traffic, so at six o'clock Saturday morning, as the sunlight began to hit the roofs of the houses, five families simultaneously came out of their houses, filled their trunks with luggage, piled into their cars, and waved to one another as they pulled into formation. The men took turns leading, and this morning Bedelia was at the head of the line, with Father and Joey in the front and Mother and Nonna, hatless, hunched in the back.

Though the neighborhood had been making this annual mass migration for years, the route was still evolving. Each driver had his own variations, and alternatives were explored on almost every trip. Shortcuts that saved a few minutes here and there were hotly debated. Sixteenth Street through Gary, Father would say, is faster, but Fan would argue, Not if you catch that bad left turn onto 41, so during rush hour you'd better stick to the highway. They often improvised as they encountered delays at train crossings or traffic accidents, and they had developed a signal system of flashing lights, horn honks, and hand gestures by which the whole formation could change routes, or stop if necessary.

Stopping was a serious matter, of course, and the men considered the need to pee as a sign of weakness. The women complained bitterly about the infrequency of bathroom breaks.

I need a pit stop, Mother would say.

Father would shoot back, Why didn't you go before we left, I told you to go.

I DID. But I'm going to pee in my pants if we don't stop.

And so a signal would be given and the whole formation would pull into a gas station and Mother would rush to the bathroom, gesturing her apology to the other cars, but soon other women would emerge and wait outside the bathroom, their husbands having urged them to go while they had the chance because they wouldn't be stopping again. Al Zanardo had actually rigged a funnel and hose through the floor of their Studebaker's back seat for his weak-bladdered wife, Fosca, and Father often threatened Mother with a similar arrangement.

Whatever the specifics of the route, there were well-known milestones along the way. First came the scenic drive south on broad Lake Shore Drive, past the Field Museum and the Planetarium, past manicured parks and beaches, eventually past the Museum of Science and Industry and its caryatids, where Lake Shore Drive ended. Here they turned inland past the gothic towers and monuments of the University of Chicago, then turned south again for the careful drive down Cottage Grove Avenue, where even on this hot day, they rolled up all the car windows and locked all the doors.

As they went down Cottage Grove Avenue, Joey knew that they were only a few blocks from Booker T's house. As they crossed Sixty-third Street, he looked out at the busy street life in the fretted shadows of the El tracks, the shoeshine stands, the knots of older men gathered around barbecue rigs pouring out the delicious smoke that infiltrated the car's ventilation system, the storefront churches, and just past the El, the bars and jazz clubs. Joey thought about the block party, the Hawk's music, and Luther's touch on his chest. He scanned the faces along the street, hoping for a glimpse of Luther or Booker T, and wondering what he would do if he saw them, but they soon passed beyond the neighborhood. Joey hoped Booker T would be all right with the coffee runs.

Moving further south, out of the congestion of the city, the car windows remained closed as they spent a pungent half-hour passing the area they called the *puzzis*, the smellies, with the flaming towers of oil refineries on the left, and the feed yards and slaughterhouses of the meat district on the right. At last, they entered Gary, Indiana, the midpoint of their journey, and took a short detour to stop for a lunch of sorts at The Dairy Maid, their only sanctioned break.

For the kids, the Dairy Maid was the highlight of the trip. It was a one-of-a-kind ice cream parlor, not to be confused with the vastly inferior frozen custard chain called Dairy Queen. It was a big, bustling place that served nothing but ice cream. And what ice cream! As the signs proclaimed, the Dairy Maid had its own grass-fed herds of dairy cows from which all its ice cream came, ice cream of unimaginable quality in unimaginable quantity, in concoctions unlike anything available anywhere else. The kids rushed ahead to find seats at the long, gleaming counters, while the adults packed into booths. Joey managed to get a seat next to Benita, who smiled and licked her lips in anticipation.

All the kids knew the Dairy Maid menu by heart. Just as with the rides at Riverview, there was a hierarchy to the various concoctions offered, and for the past hour they had been debating their orders. For the youngest, there were simple sundaes in any one of twelve flavors of ice cream and six kinds of sauce, with embellishments like chopped nuts, melted marshmallow, and fresh strawberries, bananas, or blueberries. Most kids, however, opted for one of the three house specialties. First, there was the Tub O'Malt. It came in a glass container so large and heavy that a small kid couldn't lift it, and was made with six scoops of ice cream blended with malt and either vanilla, chocolate, fresh strawberry, or banana flavoring. Next was the Parfait, weighing in at eight scoops, each of a different flavor, layered with various sauces, and the whole topped by an extraordinary mound of real whipped cream, nuts, and a cherry. At the pinnacle of the Dairy Maid menu was the Banana Boat, which was to an ordinary banana split as a mole hill was to the great Pyramid of Cheops, which, in fact, it resembled; it had the ten scoops of ice cream piled in layers with four balls of vanilla at the bottom, three of chocolate next, then two of strawberry plus another on top. Nestled on either side of this mound of ice cream were halves of two bananas, various sauces and fresh fruit, and a covering of whipped cream. Few kids had ever finished a Banana Boat, and parents were slow to order it, saying, You'll never finish it, and you'll get a stomach ache if you do. Joey had never even attempted a Banana Boat and was wavering between a Tub O'Malt and a Parfait, when Benita turned to him with a wicked smile and said, The Banana Boat. He knew instinctively that the time had come for him to pay for his betrayal in Aladdin's Castle, and speaking to him for the first time since that infamous day, she again uttered the fateful words, I dare you.

A murmur ran up and down the counter as the kids all turned to look at Joey, who gathered himself to meet the challenge. The order was given. Expectation mounted as the clerk built the impressive concoction, then hefted it onto the counter in front of Joey. Spoonful by spoonful, Joey dug at the mountain of ice cream, watched intently by all the other kids. His mother kept clucking and shaking her head, muttering, You're going to be sorry, don't complain to me. As the last spoonful was making its reluctant way toward his stomach, everybody cheered. Joey managed a faint smile, being careful not to open his mouth too much. As they left, Joey walked carefully. Benita smiled at him expectantly.

After the Dairy Maid, it was traditional for the kids to switch cars when they resumed the journey to Stevensville, which was another hour and a half away, and Benita invited Joey to ride with her and Peter in Fan's big Oldsmobile. She looked expectantly at Joey as they drove on, through the little piece of Indiana that sat at the bottom of the Lake, and well into Michigan. Joey smiled at her, wondering what it was she expected from him. His smile grew fainter and fainter during the hour it took to reach New Buffalo, Michigan, and on a desolate stretch of road outside of town he finally asked them to stop the car. He jumped out, knelt ignominiously at the side of the road, and gave the Banana Boat back to the grass from whence it had come. Wiping his mouth, he took his place in the back of the car next to a smirking Peter. As they pulled away, Joey glanced across at Benita. She sat upright, her hands folded in her lap, a faint smile on her lips, staring straight ahead in quiet satisfaction, her revenge complete.

19

STEVENSVILLE

AT LAST THEY TURNED OFF HIGHWAY 41 onto a rough, macadam-covered street called Glenlord Road, an unmarked little byway in the deep shade of a tunnel of elm trees. Whoever Steven had been, his accomplishments must have been modest, for his namesake had only one street and its downtown consisted of only two buildings next to a railroad crossing. Stretching down Glenlord Road from the crossing, half-hidden in the grape vines and bushes beyond the line of elms, were a number of small summer houses. Most of these had been built by families from the West Side, and though they were simple and small, they were sources of great pride to their owners, as if they were the lost villas of old Tuscany.

Not every family enjoyed the luxury of their own summer house, of course, and those that didn't stayed in one of two places, which, though they were little more than makeshift collections of bedrooms around a communal kitchen, were grandly called resorts. The larger of the two was Parmentoni's Resort, belonging to cousin

Paula's family of pasta-makers, a two-storied former schoolhouse covered with dark brown wooden shingles and surrounded by large elm trees in which a network of walkways and stairs led to various platforms and small tree houses. Joey loved this tree world, but he had to content himself with only visiting Benita here, for his family always stayed instead at Rita's Resort, a smaller complex owned by a great-aunt farther down Glenlord Road toward the beach.

Rita's Resort was a converted farmhouse with a vineyard in back. The main building was long and low and covered with broad, white asbestos shingles. Inside were two small bedrooms that shared one bathroom, and two large dormitories, each with six beds, sharing one large bathroom. In the front of the building was the communal kitchen. Out back there was a smaller building with a functioning windmill on one side, a shed, a chicken yard, a garden, and long rows of grapevines that were still cultivated. The smaller building had once been a garage and was now converted to a bedroom with a washhouse and toilet along one side. It was in this room, still called the garage, that Joey and his family always stayed. Inside there were two beds, one for his parents and one for Nonna, and a fold-up cot for Joey, all so tightly packed into the room that you could barely walk between them. Joey and Father carried the suitcases in and arranged them on the beds for unpacking. There was no closet, so clothes were hung from rows of coat hooks along two walls. Underwear, socks, and such were stuffed into one old dresser with a broken front leg supported by an empty grape crate.

After they were settled, Joey heard a commotion behind the garage and went out to investigate. In back of the windmill, in the large garden that serviced the resort, Rita herself, a small, sturdy woman with a grizzled chin, wearing an old flowered housedress, a small axe in her hand, was chasing one of the chickens that ran freely among the pole beans, zucchini, lettuce, and tomato plants. She soon caught it, and carried it squawking and flapping to a tree stump at the base of the windmill tower. A quick stroke of the axe and the head fell to the ground. She released the body and Joey was amazed to see it run around the yard headless for many minutes. Rita laughed at his dismay, and said, *e buono loro fanno che, aiuta a pulirli*, it's good they do that, it helps clean them out. When the chicken faltered, she picked it up by the feet and hung it upside down from one of the crossbars of the windmill tower, where two other headless chickens already hung, twitching. Joey stared at the three birds hanging like Christ and the two thieves. Rita saw the outrage in his eyes, and in justification explained that hanging like this, they would bleed themselves out and drain their stomachs, saving a lot of messy work and making the meat tastier. In a few hours they would be ready to cook for dinner.

Joey left the site of the atrocity and wandered out through the grapevines. Birds flew from tree to tree with bits of grass and twigs in their beaks, building nests. Atop one of the posts that supported the grapevines he found a small nest with three tiny eggs. He guessed it must be a hummingbird nest and was careful not to disturb it.

He emerged from the vineyard at the little creek that ran behind the property. He was glad to see that the water was running well, for by the end of summer it sometimes dried up. Low sumac trees and willow bushes grew thickly along the banks, and a barely discernible path led along the creek to a small clearing guarded by stinging nettles. He had discovered this spot the previous summer and had prepared it as a secret retreat, dragging in a large fallen branch to use as a seat. He was relieved to see that the log remained just as he had left it last summer. He rolled it over and retrieved the coffee can he had hidden in a hole under it. In it were several pages torn from the lingerie section of an old Sears and Roebuck catalog, but they were wet and had matted together. He carried stones from along the bank and repaired the small dam he had built last summer, forming a backwater deep enough to dangle his feet in. He sat for a long time, listening to the running water, bird songs, and the wind in the sumac trees, and smelling the dampness of the grasses. A small, striped snake slithered through the grass. The basement flat and dirty cement of Chicago began to fade from his memory.

He caught a gnarled toad that came hopping through the clearing, and as he held it in his palm, it wet him. Bruno had told him that toad urine caused warts, so he quickly released it and washed his hands vigorously in the stream. As he was wiping his hands on his pants, he heard the distant wail of a train whistle. In great excitement, he ran back along the creek and went through the vineyard by a circuitous route that would keep the location of his hideout secret from any onlookers. As he emerged from the vines, he saw that the crucified chickens had been taken down. He ran past the main building and out onto Glenlord Road.

The railroad crossing that defined the town was only a few hundred feet from Rita's front door. Four times each day, steam locomotives passed, pulling long trains of boxcars and automobile carriers from Detroit bound for Chicago. All the kids eagerly anticipated a train's approach, and Joey was soon joined by Bruno and Big Paulie, who were also staying at Rita's. The three of them ran onto the tracks and saw a plume of black smoke already rising above the line of trees on the horizon. Bruno bent down and put his ear on the track. Listen! he said, you can hear it coming, and Joey and Big Paulie knelt too. The cold iron track began to tremble.

Yes, I hear it! Joey cried, It's a kind of grinding noise. The solitary cross-armed signal at the crossing began to flash its red lights and ring its insistent bell.

Quick, Bruno said, pennies! They searched their pockets and found five pennies among them. Placing them carefully on the track, Joey and Bruno retreated to the edge of the gravel roadbed. Despite the fervent warnings of their parents, they tried to get as close to the passing train as they dared, and Big Paulie lingered on the track until the belching black monster was almost upon them, the ground shaking, the whistle deafening. Bruno yelled, Get the hell out of there, you stupid shit! Just in time, Big Paulie scrambled down beside them, and they covered their ears and shut their eyes against the swirling dust as the train thundered past at tremendous speed, the ties bending and groaning under the weight, the wheels clacking on the joints in the track. Box cars, tank cars, empty openwork cattle cars, refrigerator cars, automobile carriers filled with new cars, all sped past, emblazoned with exotic names from other places, like Santa Fe, C&NW, The Belt Line, Denver & Rio Grande. Out loud they counted the cars, thirty-nine, forty, forty-one. When they reached sixty-four, the noise diminished and they looked up in time to wave at the brakeman who sat in the little bay window of the caboose smoking his pipe. As the train raced away, they came forward and pried the pennies up, now squashed into long ovals. Bruno swatted Big Paulie on the back of the head, saying, That was really dumb, imagine what that train would do to you.

They walked out onto the road. On one side of the crossing was Schulz's market, a small general store opened years ago by one of the few German immigrant families that had settled in the area. Mrs. Schulz was a jolly, fat woman who sometimes gave kids penny candy, but her husband was grizzled and stern. He quickly sent kids packing if they didn't have money in their hands. You could never be sure which Schulz might be tending the store at a given time, and not wanting to risk the luck of the draw, the three of them headed instead across the tracks to their favorite hangout, the second of the two buildings that comprised greater metropolitan Stevensville, Harvey Seasongood's Emporium and Scale.

The concrete block building had a corrugated metal roof and a loading dock on the side next to the tracks. In front of the loading dock was the large truck scale that once had weighed shipments of peaches and Concord grapes grown in the area, the iron scale mechanism still standing black in the sun with its lever arm and hanging weights. Harvey's scale was long-since overgrown with thistles and milkweed because nowadays the grapes were collected by trucks from the House of David, the Ultra-orthodox Jewish organization that owned most of the vineyards and orchards in southern Michigan, and produced jam, jelly, sweet Concord wine, and a famous baseball team. The three boys crossed the defunct scale, jumping up and down to see if the mechanism would still move, which it wouldn't, and went inside.

Harvey Seasongood's Emporium was cool and dark. In the front room there was a small glass case stocked with stale candy bars, jars full of ropes of red and black licorice, paper tapes studded with candy dots, and fishing gear. Against one wall was a red metal cooler filled with ice water from which, after putting a nickel in a jar, you could pull a frosty glass bottle of the local soda pops, like Vernor's Original Ginger Ale, Nehi Strawberry, Orange Crush, or Dad's Old Fashioned Honey-Lemon Root Beer.

In the center of the large back room was a big potbelly stove which Joey had never seen lit. In a circle around it were six ancient leather swivel armchairs, and in one of them sat Harvey Seasongood himself, a wizened and wise old man whose perpetual smile personified his name. In three of the other chairs sat other local men of Harvey's vintage, as they did most afternoons and evenings, spinning yarns, chewing tobacco, and spitting expertly into the unpolished brass cuspidor next to the stove, which Harvey called simply the spittoon.

Harvey looked up as the three boys came in, smiled and said, Well, hello, I see the Mafia is back for another summer, my, ain't you gettin' big!

The boys loved Harvey and were glad to see he had lasted another year. Hi, Harvey, they all sang in unison, and Joey asked, Could I pay for a soda with these squashed pennies?

Sure, Harvey said, it's all legal tender no matter what shape it's in, you can even send in bills that have gotten tored up or burnt and they'll pay ya' for 'em. Joey went back into the front room, dropped the elongated pennies into the jar, and fished around up to the elbow in the frigid water of the cooler until he found his favorite, a bottle of Green River.

Bruno and Big Paulie had already gone to the side room where there was a pool table as old as Harvey, on which Bruno had last summer taught Joey the rudiments of the game. The cues were warped and most lacked tips, so there was no need for chalk. The table's green felt was frayed and mended from years of misuse by children, and two of the leather pockets were broken out so the chipped ivory balls fell from them to the concrete floor. Harvey never charged the kids for playing pool, regarding it as an essential part of a proper upbringing. The boys were in the middle of a game of Rotation when they heard from across the street the clanging of the dinner bell, salvaged from an old fire truck, that Rita used to call her guests to the table.

The boys said goodbye to Harvey and ran across the street to join their folks and the three other families staying at Rita's that summer. They crowded into the communal kitchen, sitting at one big table, shoulder to shoulder, eighteen of them in all. At one side was the ancient wood-burning stove on which Rita did her cooking. The smell of chicken roasted with fresh sage mingled with the lingering, acrid smell of singed feathers, for it was another of Rita's culinary techniques to burn the pinfeathers off the birds over an open flame after plucking. The chicken was accompanied by fresh produce from the garden, string beans, zucchini, and a salad of dark green bitter escarole and *radicchio*, laced with sliced fresh tomatoes. Clear, unlabeled bottles of homemade red wine had been filled from the barrel in the shed beneath the windmill. The only item on the menu not produced on the property was the bread brought all the way from Fontana's, the supply being replenished every week by the fathers who went back and forth to work in the city.

Everyone lingered at the table for hours after the last of the food had been consumed, sipping wine and chatting through a blue haze of cigarette smoke as the latest news from each family and from the old country was shared. Even the children sat happily, enveloped in the warmth of this summer's extended family. At last, Nonna Severina, as the reigning matriarch of the group, hauled her generous bulk up from the table and announced, *Io sono stanco, è stato un giorno lungo e l'aria di paese mi fa sonnolento, il letto si sentirà bene*, I'm tired, it's been a long day and the country air makes me sleepy, the bed will feel good. Everyone took their cue and the families began a short version of the traditional Long Goodbye that lasted only twenty minutes or so. Soon everyone moved off down the long central hallway of the main building toward their respective bedrooms, while Joey and his family went out the kitchen door and walked across the yard to the garage.

Mother and Nonna went inside to put on their nightgowns. Joey and Father took their turn in the washhouse that had been added to the side of the garage. It was a rudimentary, uninsulated structure that ran the length of the building. It had a corrugated metal roof, and there were broad spaces between the weathered boards. The door creaked loudly and was held closed by a loop of baling wire.

Inside there was a single bare light bulb with a pull chain over an old porcelain sink that hung askew on the inside wall. Above the sink, two garden faucets were screwed to the wall, and the exposed iron pipes led to the propane hot water heater that sat just outside. A tub-style Bendix washing machine stood beside the sink with black rubber hoses attached to the water lines, and a drain hose hooked over the edge of the sink. The Bendix had a wringer mounted on one side, a frame containing two cracked, white rubber rollers with a pressure adjustment, and a handle that turned the rollers. There was a rusted metal shower stall at one end, with a plastic curtain gathered on a metal rod. Beside it, raised on an uneven platform, was a toilet hidden behind a partial door.

While his father was in the toilet, Joey stuck his finger between the rollers on the Bendix and turned the crank. His finger was sucked in and painfully squeezed, and he cried out in surprise when the handle would not turn in reverse. He stood there shamefaced until Father came out and released the safety catch that opened the rollers. Well, Father said, I guess you know not to do that again. It's your turn in the toilet. Joey went in while his father plugged his electric razor into the socket on the side of the light fixture. Joey had noticed that his father always shaved at night before going to bed. From inside the toilet he asked, Dad, why do you shave at night instead of in the morning?

Your mother, Father replied with his lips drawn tight as he stuck out his chin and ran the razor up and down his neck. She doesn't like to get scraped by my beard in bed.

Listening to the hypnotic buzz of his father's shaver, Joey sat on the toilet's cracked wooden seat, peeking out into the yard through gaps in the wall, enjoying the thrill of shitting nearly al fresco. When he was done, as he rocked to one side to wipe himself, he looked up and saw a huge, speckled, orange garden spider hanging in a web directly overhead just inches away. Garden spiders were common here and Joey knew they weren't dangerous, but the extraordinary size of this one was startling. He decided not to mention it to the others.

Back inside the garage, Joey and his father undressed and pulled on their flannel pajamas while Mother and Nonna went out to use the washroom. Joey snuggled into his cot and waited. The scream came quickly. *Oh Dio, che bestia!* Nonna cried, and his mother yelled, Dino, come quick, a spider! Father rushed out, and Joey listened to the women's hysterical voices and the repeated blows of a broom as his father dispatched the unfortunate spider. Finally it was quiet and everyone came back in.

As she got into bed, Mother looked over at Joey and said, Be sure to look around when you go in that toilet, you could get eaten alive. Joey promised he would.

Joey's cot was pushed right against his grandmother's bed. After they were all tucked in, the chenille bedspreads pulled up to their chins against the night chill, Nonna leaned close to him and began softly to sing a lullaby.

Michaele-le, Michaele-le, aveva un cane piccolo.
Rososo e biancoco, un vero tombolino-no.
E per mangiare dava, Minestre ed pananele-le,
Viva Michaele-le, viva Michaele-le.

Little Michael, Little Michael, had a little dog.
It was pink and white, a real clown.
And to eat, Michael gave it soup and bread.
Hooray for Michael, hooray for Michael.

Joey's mother said softly, *Io ricordo colui, Ma, Lei lo cantava a me quando io ero picin.* I remember that one, Ma, you used to sing it to me when I was little.

Sì, io facevo, Yes, I did, Nonna whispered, *Era Suo favorito,* It was your favorite.

Then it was quiet. Joey could hear the adults breathing and the murmur of insects outside. A dog barked far away. A car passed slowly, its headlights wiping lazily across the windows, throwing patterns on the bowed ceiling. Bedsprings creaked, then quieted. Soon a chorus of snoring filled the room. His father was the baritone, with long, lyrical phrases. His mother was the soprano, with staccato bursts. Under both was the surprising basso profundo of his grandmother, the biggest pipe in the organ. Joey couldn't resist sitting up on his cot and conducting, as he did the opera records at home. He let his family's music swirl around him like a warm blanket. Then he laid back, content and safe, and despite the noise was soon deep in a blessedly dreamless sleep.

20 DEATH IN THE VINEYARD

THE MOURNING DOVES COOED SO LOUDLY THEY WOKE JOEY EARLY. He lay in his cot, listening. The chill of the night was gone, and the sun had warmed the air. Dust motes danced in the yellow light that filtered through the cloth window shades. It was Sunday morning, but there were no church bells calling the faithful to Mass. Even God, Joey thought, needed a summer vacation. His folks were still asleep, but the chorus of snoring had diminished to heavy breathing. Joey got up quietly. He took his clothes and shoes from the chair where he had put them the night before, went out, barefoot, and dressed in the washhouse. Though the spider in the toilet was gone, halfway up the windmill tower outside he saw another against the rising sun, a big one sitting still in its web on which drops of dew glistened like jewels in the light.

The low, bright sunlight made the windmill glow. The faded lettering on the tail that said Aeromotor was still legible as it swung lazily, finding the wind. There was just enough breeze to move the vanes. Joey traced the action of the machine with his eyes. The windmill turned a lever that lifted a long rod, up and down, up and down. This was attached at the bottom to the handle of a cast iron water pump that rose and fell, rose and fell. Sparkling water spurted from the iron spout and collected in a corrugated trough, from which the overflow ran into ditches that watered the garden plants.

In a shed next to the windmill there was an electric pump that drew from the same well. As Joey looked in, it clicked on and whirred, pumping water into a galvanized pressure tank from which pipes led to the washhouse, then to the main house. Next to the tank was a workbench. Hanging on the wall behind the bench were old tools that had been used by Rita's husband when he was alive, but now sat rusting. Joey picked up a plane, its wooden handle rich with the oil of years of working fingers. There were mallets, long chisels, thick clamps with wooden screws, and saws of myriad shapes. Joey was considering what he might build with these wondrous tools when he noticed, leaning against the workbench, an old BB gun. Joey picked it up. The barrel was rusty, and the varnish had peeled off the wooden stock. Joey shook the gun and it rattled, so he knew there were pellets in the tube that ran under the barrel. He stepped out of the shed and cocked the lever. He aimed at the surface of the water trough and pulled the trigger. Splash!

Joey cocked the gun and tucked it under his arm. He wandered back between the grape vines, enjoying the morning light. He saw a striped snake gliding through the wet grass. He raised the gun and sighted toward the snake, but to one side. Snap! The grass moved as the BB cut through it, fully three feet from the snake, which quickly slithered out of sight. Joey walked on, shooting at bunches of grapes, a rag hanging in a tree, and a rusty can. He hit none of them. Then a plump mourning dove fluttered in and landed on one of the grape posts, about thirty feet away. Joey cocked the gun and pointed it in the general direction of the bird, not bothering to aim carefully. He remembered the slaughter of the blackbird hunt and was glad the BB gun was harmless. He pulled the trigger. Snap! The bird fluttered a few feet straight up, and to Joey's horror, fell flopping between the vines. He ran to where it was thrashing in the grass. He tried to lift it, to help it fly, but it only struggled harder. After a few moments, it lay in the grass and only jerked and twitched. Joey realized it was dying and in pain. He remembered how his father had taught him to hold wounded birds by the head and flick the bodies, breaking the neck. He lifted the dove and looked into its eyes. He couldn't bring himself to kill it. He laid it back gently in the grass and watched the little, rapid movements of its breast rising and falling. He was still watching it when Rita rang the first bell for Sunday brunch.

On weekdays, the communal breakfast was served around eight. It was a simple meal, the central ingredient being dark, pungent, espresso coffee with the potency of varnish remover, served in huge mugs with cream or scalded milk. Coffee was served to everyone, young and old, though the youngsters got theirs much diluted with milk. Rita brewed her coffee in a huge, dark-blue enameled steel pot. She put the grounds loose in the bottom of the pot, then broke an egg and dropped the white, shell and all, atop them. The whole thing was then brought to the boil for several minutes. In theory, the egg whites were supposed to form a layer that would filter out the grounds, in the same way that egg white was used to filter wine in the old country. But in practice, what Rita produced was a coffee stew in which, as Father said, you had to tie your keys to a cube of sugar to make it sink. It was important to slurp a little gently off the surface in order to avoid a mouthful of grounds, and sixteen people drinking Rita's coffee was a noisy affair. The coffee was accompanied by platters of thick slices of Tuscan bread toasted in the big black iron skillet, and large pots of sweet butter and homemade apple, pear, and, of course, Concord grape jelly.

Sunday brunch was a very different affair, not just because it was served later, around ten, and was a much more substantial meal than weekday breakfasts, but because all the fathers would be leaving a few hours after the meal. They worked all week, and when they finished work on Friday they left directly from their jobs, drove through the rush hour, and arrived in Stevensville after dark for a late dinner. They spent all day Saturday with their families, and after brunch on Sunday returned again to the city. This weekly migration lasted all summer, and Sunday brunch was a sort of bon voyage party to fortify the fathers for the trip and comfort the mothers and children left behind. It consisted of platters full of scrambled eggs brought fresh from the chicken yard, slabs of thick Italian ham, mounds of sweet sausages, bowls of fresh fruit salad, all accompanying a large serving of roast meat.

On this first Sunday, unfortunately for Joey, the main course was a platter of roast squabs that Rita's son Raymond had shot the week before. Rita prepared squabs as she had in the old country, roasted whole with the heads left on, submerged in a thick tomato sauce. Joey stared at the birds on the platter, their limp heads dangling, and could see only the dove twitching in the wet grass between the grape vines. His heart felt like a lump of cold mud in his chest. What's the matter, Joey? Mother said. You're not eating, do you feel sick?

Everyone looked up. In this family a poor appetite was a sure symptom of a serious illness. Nonna reached over and felt Joey's forehead. *Lui ha un poco caldo*, He's a little warm, she said gravely.

Joey was embarrassed and irritated by the attention. No, he said, I don't have a fever, I'm fine, just not hungry.

Mother asked, Did you go this morning? Maybe you're constipated.

No, Joey snapped, I'm not constipated.

Rita herself came over to examine the patient. She felt the glands in Joey's neck, her calloused fingers scraping his skin. *Io so ciò del quale lui ha bisogn,* I know what he needs, she said.

She went to the cupboard and got down a big bottle of Martini and Rossi Sweet Vermouth. She rinsed out a glass and poured Joey a healthy slug. *Questo riparerà Lei diritto su*, this'll fix you right up, she said, and put it to Joey's lips. He drank, the sweet liquid warming its way to his stomach. Good, he said, and meant it.

Rita poured a little more. Mother said, Not so much. But Rita insisted that it would do him good. Joey drank, and the warmth of the sweet liquid rose from his stomach to his head.

I feel better already, he said.

Ecco! Rita was triumphant.

Joey got up and said, I think I'll just go and play now.

Fine, everyone said, relieved at his recovery.

Be careful, Mother said, it's still chilly out this early.

Oh, leave the boy alone, said Father.

Joey ran back to the vineyard, his stomach fluttering with Vermouth and fear. As he approached, he could see the depression in the grass where the bird had fallen. He slowed and walked, step by step, toward it, seeing it as if through someone else's eyes. The bird was still, the little claws in the air, the head hanging grotesquely to one side like the squabs on the platter. Joey put his hand under the body and lifted it. It was so light, and already cold and hard. He carried it back to his secret clearing by the creek. He laid it aside and rolled the log over. He lifted the coffee can out of its hollow and shook out the matted Sears and Roebuck girdle pictures. He carefully put the bird in the can, then used a stick to make the hollow deeper.

As he dug, he began to cry. He tried to hold back, but his tears only came harder. By the time he laid the entombed bird in the hole, his body was wracked with sobs. Barely able to see, he pushed the earth back over the can, seeing again the casket closing over his Nonno Lorenzo, saying what he had been unable to say that day in Anzilotti's parlor, Goodbye, goodbye, Nonno, Nonno, I love you. He ran all the way back to the garage, stumbling against the posts in the vineyard. He threw open the door of their bedroom and saw his father closing his suitcase.

What is it? Father asked, alarmed. Joey ran to him and held him as tight as he could. What's wrong? Father asked again.

Joey sobbed, Don't die, you mustn't die.

No, Father said, I'm not going to die, not for a long time anyway. Not for a very long time.

Later that day, all the fathers gathered for the trip back to Chicago. They shared three of the cars, leaving the others behind for their families. Bedelia was one of those that made the trip, and Father got behind the wheel as Big Paulie's father and two others climbed in. Joey and the other kids stood beside their mothers as the cars pulled out. Bedelia was the last in line. Joey and Mother waved, and Father waved back. Joey sniffled.

It's just a week, Mother said, he'll be back on Friday.

21 THE HOUSE OF DAVID

THE THREE BOYS STAYING AT RITA'S THAT SUMMER, Bruno, Big Paulie, and Joey, were inseparable and came to be called *La banda della vita corta*, which meant loosely, the Gang with a Short Life, or better, the Gang that Lived Dangerously. The two girls staying at Rita's, Joey's second cousins Arlene and Geraldine, were younger and spent their time with their mothers, but the three boys ranged further and further afield, escaping from the watchfulness of their mothers and grandmothers. When they were not at the beach, they played pool at Harvey Seasongood's. When they were tired of that, they went foraging like wild animals, eating grapes that were not yet ripe and peaches that were still hard, and getting stomach aches. At least the wild raspberries, red and black, that grew in abundance at the side of the road near Parmentoni's Resort, were ripe, though Joey once forgot to check for burrs and got one stuck on his tongue. These simple pleasures filled their days.

The nighttime recreational choices in Stevensville were limited to say the least, and some inventiveness was required. Frogs were hunted by flashlight, bonfires were held on the beach, hide and seek was played in the treetop walkways at the Parmentoni Resort, and once or twice a month the kids were taken to the Starlight drive-in movie at the junction of Glenlord Road and Highway 41. The Starlight charged by the carload, so everyone piled into two cars, one from each resort.

The car from Rita's was driven by Rita's son, Raymond. The kids all liked Raymond, a soft-spoken, pleasant man with a pencil-line mustache. Though he was only in his mid-twenties, he seemed older. He was a bachelor and often served as babysitter. Father told Joey with real pride that Ray had joined the Canadian army early, even before America had entered World War II, and had been a bombardier in the Air Force. Father said that sometimes Ray drank too much because of something that had happened in the war. The kids asked Ray about it, but he only shrugged and said, That's over with. Years later Ray would drink himself to death, but at the Starlight, he was accepted as one of the gang. Ray's car carried Joey, Bruno, Big Paulie, Arlene and Geraldine. The car from the Parmentoni Resort carried Fosca, Anna, Delia, and Francesca, cousins so distant that Joey could not follow the genealogy when his mother recited it. Most important, the Parmentoni car also carried Peter and Benita.

The movie didn't start until it was dark, and at this time of the year it didn't get dark until after nine, so they arrived early and the kids congregated in the playground at the base of the big white screen. They saw each other almost every day at the beach, but the time at the Starlight was special because, except for Ray and the other driver, there were no adults to watch over them and they made the most of their freedom. When the picture finally started they ran back to the cars and unfolded aluminum garden chairs, or spread blankets on the sandy ground, and pulled the speakers on the iron posts as close as possible. The Starlight couldn't afford first-run features, so the kids saw a lot of old movies, usually horror films like Joey's favorites, *Curse of the Cat People* and *The Picture of Dorian Gray,* interspersed with family movies like *National Velvet, The Best Years of Our Lives*, and *The Bells of St. Mary's.* Whenever a movie lapsed into romance, and especially during kissing scenes, the boys would whoop and run around and dash through the projector beam, while the girls shushed them and watched in starry-eyed fascination. At intermission the boys ran to be first in line at the concrete blockhouse that served as both projection booth and concession stand, and the girls, particularly Benita, would run to get in the long line outside the one toilet that served the entire Coke-swilling horde.

On other Saturdays, special excursions were held as the grandparents conspired to keep the children as far away from the resorts for as long as possible, this being the only night of the week that the fathers and mothers could be alone to enjoy a conjugal visit. At least twice each summer the kids were taken to a baseball game at the House of David, and afterward to the small amusement park that was part of the House of David complex. For kids weaned on Riverview's Bobs and Parachutes, and compared even to the amusement park in St. Joe called Silver Beach, the House of David Park was barely tolerable. The most exciting ride was a miniature steam train so small that even Joey had to tuck his knees up in the open car as it wound past scenes from the Old Testament, including Noah's Ark tossing on a painted Flood, Lot's wife tottering as a pillar of salt, and as a climax, a Burning Bush that emitted a brief gas flame. In addition to the train ride, there was a small carousel, a row of distorting mirrors, and a grove of picnic tables under garlands of colored lights. Here kosher hot dogs, schooners of beer, or glasses of sweet Concord wine were sold, the limits of moderation being strictly enforced by the House of David members, stout and imposing men with full beards in black suits, white shirts without collars, and broad-brimmed black hats.

The House of David Park had one redeeming feature. In a large, open-air pavilion of ornate iron, there were rows and rows of old pinball machines and other hand-operated games. Even the newest and most elaborate of these were of pre-war vintage, and had illuminated displays of painted glass or rows of flashing light bulbs. Some of the games were antiques dating from an era before electricity, mechanical marvels that fascinated Joey. There were penny movies in which you looked through an eyepiece and turned a crank that fanned a row of black and white photos showing someone getting hit by a pie, falling down stairs, or escaping from an oncoming train. Though Joey had heard of penny movies with risqué subjects, those at the House of David offered scenes of impeccable rectitude. There were also baseball games and golfing games and Skee Ball. Best of all, there were true pinball games in which steel ball bearings rolled down tilted tables, hitting not the flashing electrical bumpers of today's machines, but pinging off nails – the pins of pinball – and ending up at the bottom in bins of varying values that collectively totaled the player's score. These machines had no tilt mechanism, so the kids lifted and wiggled them enthusiastically until one of the stern members of the House of David glared in their direction.

Standing outside the pinball pavilion was a row of fortune-telling machines. One had a bust of a turbaned prophet named Swami Knowall Tellall, who, when a coin was inserted and a lever pressed, turned his head, blinked his eyes, opened his mouth, and spit out a fortune printed on a strip of cardboard. Joey got one that said, *You will find your one true love tonight.* He made the mistake of showing it to Big Paulie, who of course told the others. They all kidded Benita and Joey about the prophecy for weeks after, until the two star-crossed lovers began, each in their private heart, to take it seriously. By the Fourth of July, they were both wracked by full-blown but entirely secret pangs of first love.

On the Fourth of July, everyone went to the Starlight Drive-in for its annual fireworks extravaganza, consisting of a showing of James Cagney in *Yankee Doodle Dandy*, followed by a fireworks American Flag, Statue of Liberty, and red, white, and blue pinwheels mounted on the playground equipment at the base of the screen. After the show, all the families gathered in the yard at Parmentoni's Resort and lit cone fountains and small firecrackers, and the kids ran across the catwalks from tree house to tree house with sparklers while the parents yelled for them not to burn everything down.

From the very highest tree perch, Joey and Benita sat, their legs touching and their feet dangling over the edge, looking down. A radio played patriotic music and the sparklers were mingled with fireflies. It seemed to Joey that this was how life was supposed to be forever.

22 CATFISH HEROES

Every Saturday morning Rita served a late breakfast for the fathers who had driven in from the city the night before. After breakfast, the reunited families would pack a picnic lunch and spend all day at the beach.

But one Saturday in mid-July, Father decided to take Joey fishing. That morning, Father shook Joey awake before dawn, and they crept silently out of the garage and dressed in the washhouse. They went into the chicken yard, where the ground was rich, and dug for earthworms, great squiggly ones they put in a coffee can. In the shed beside the windmill were some simple bamboo poles with hooks, line, weights and bobbers, and they chose two and slipped them into Bedelia, the long poles sticking out of a partially open front window.

They drove the half hour up the highway, deserted at this hour, to the city of St. Joe lurking in the gray predawn light. They turned off the highway onto a side street and stopped on the bridge where the St. Joe River emptied into Lake Michigan. A few other fishermen were already on the bridge, most of them older black men, with their lines disappearing into the wisps of fog that hung over the water. The sun was just coming up as Joey unwound the lines from the bamboo poles. Father showed Joey how to bait his hook so that the worm remained alive, thrashing in a way that no fish could resist, attach a weight, and set the bobber to the proper depth.

They dropped in their lines as the sun slanted across the water and the fog evaporated. The air was still, the whole city silent. The fishermen were hunched at the railing, some smoking, some sipping coffee from thermoses, staring down at their bobbers. After a time, Father's pole jerked, his bobber disappeared, there was splashing below, and up came a fish, a small, flat fish that Father said was a bluegill, Not very good eating, we'll throw it back. Father pulled out the hook and a stain of red covered the fish's mouth. Remembering the dove, Joey was alarmed and asked, Does it hurt them?

No, they don't feel a thing, Father answered, it'll be fine. And sure enough, as soon as it hit the water, the little fish revived and disappeared in a flash of silver. Joey was relieved.

The sun was higher when Joey felt a tremendous tug, his bobber disappeared with a splash, and his bamboo pole bent until it might snap. Set it, set the hook, Father cried. Joey gave a tug, his heart pounding. Good, Father said, now pull it in, steady or you'll break the line. Joey lifted the bamboo pole until he could grab the line in his hands and heaved until he pulled up a huge, shiny black fish with a big gaping mouth and long whiskers.

The old black man fishing beside them looked over and said, That's a mighty fine catfish, young man.

Joey pulled it over the railing and it flopped around at their feet. Joey reached for it and, too late, Father said, Watch out! One of the whiskers pierced Joey's hand. It had barbs on it, and the more Joey struggled against it, the deeper it penetrated. The pain was terrific, but Joey clenched his teeth and refused to cry.

The old black man said, My, my, that can hurt. He reached into his tackle box and took out a pair of rusty pliers. Here, he said, I use these.

Father took the pliers and grasped the whisker. Ready? he asked. Joey grunted through his clenched teeth and closed his eyes. There was a searing pain, but the whisker came out.

The old black man handed over a small bottle of iodine and said, Here, best get this on or it'll get infected, this river's pretty dirty.

Father took it and applied the iodine, which stung. Father blew on the wound, saying, The stinging is good, it means it's working. He wrapped his handkerchief around Joey's hand, then gave the pliers and iodine back to the old black man and said, Thanks a lot. Then he ran a stringer through the fish's mouth and out the gills and put it back in the water, where he said it would keep fresh.

By noon they had more than a dozen huge catfish on the stringer, enough to feed everyone at Rita's. As they packed up, the old black man said, A fine day, young man, you got a good catch. Those'll be real good fried in batter, have 'em with some greens. Father smiled and said that was just what they would do.

On the way home, they stopped at a roadside stand in the black section of St. Joe and bought a bunch of mustard greens. As they drove away, Father said, Niggers really know their catfish, one of them at work taught me how to cook it and it's the best fish you'll ever want to eat.

When Rita saw the catfish, she crinkled up her nose and said, *Mangiatori di immondizia! Li trovi fuori della mia cucina!* Garbage eaters! Get them out of my kitchen! So Father and Joey went out back to the windmill to clean the catfish themselves. Father set a wooden board on the ground next to the water trough and showed Joey how to gut and clean the fish. After the heads were cut off and the barbed whiskers were no longer a threat, Joey actually enjoyed pulling out the handfuls of entrails and bladders. Father filleted the bodies with a sharp knife. The tails, spines, heads, and guts went into a bucket, and Joey was sent to bury them in the soft soil between the grape vines, where Father assured him they would be good fertilizer.

That night, over Rita's objections, Father coated the catfish filets in flour, dipped them in a mixture of egg and water, then rolled them in seasoned bread crumbs. They were deep-fried in a big pot of very hot corn oil. While they cooked, Joey and Father recounted their fishing adventure, and Joey displayed his injured hand to much sympathy and adulation. The fish came out brown and crispy on the outside and succulent on the inside, and were served, just as the old black man had suggested, with the cooked mustard greens with a dash of vinegar. Everyone who tasted them thought they were quite wonderful, although Rita and Nonna refused to put what they considered *pesce di Neri*, nigger fish, in their mouths.

The two old women said this without malice, as a matter of simple fact, but it made Joey sad, and in a way he didn't yet fully understand, angry. Remembering their conversation on the El, Joey looked over at Bruno, who sat across from him.

Bruno's eyes told him that he understood what Joey was feeling, but he gave his head a little shake, sadly, saying in effect, I know, but now is not the time or place for a discussion of racial tolerance.

Joey took a deep breath, then a big mouthful of catfish, and chewed in silence.

23 PERVERSION IN THE SUMACS

ONE AFTERNOON IN LATE JULY, Big Paulie had a bad sunburn and was prohibited from the beach, so the whole gang of three stayed home. Playing pool and foraging had long since grown tiresome. In desperation, Joey, against his better judgment, offered to take them all to his secret place. He led them through the vineyard back to the already diminished creek, along the path, and into his clearing. The sumac trees were in full foliage and hung over the clearing like a canopy, making it seem even more secret. Here the three of them sat and, as boys will, soon started to talk about girls.

Bruno, as the oldest, might have been expected to take the lead, but since he had by then publicly announced his intention to enter the priesthood, the boys were a bit uncomfortable talking about sex in his presence. Joey, his experience so far limited to the Sears and Roebuck catalog and two kisses from Benita, was intensely curious and asked some tentative questions, wondering for example, about the odd behavior of the male member. Big Paulie, the most at ease of the three of them, laughed and said, Yeah, mine can get pretty big.

Oh, sure, Joey scoffed, yours is so big.

Big Paulie was offended. Well, it is, he said, bigger than yours, that's for sure.

Though his heart was not in it, Joey felt obliged to say, I bet it's not. Joey was, in fact, secretly afraid that his penis was too small. In the bathtub, he had discovered that, being chubby, he could make it disappear altogether by tucking it up and squeezing his legs together.

But now Big Paulie was standing and unbuttoning his pants, saying, Let's just see about that!

Bruno made a hesitant noise, Now, wait a minute, guys.

But Big Paulie kept unbuttoning and said, Bruno, you be the judge, and dropped his pants and underwear.

Joey could see at once that Big Paulie was aptly named. Joey saw no point in calling the bet and tried to throw in his hand, saying, Hey, that's okay, you win.

But Big Paulie wasn't about to let him off so easily. Come on, he said, let's see what you got.

His face burning, Joey got up and dropped his pants.

Big Paulie was bending over to get a better view and laughing when Joey's mother came thrashing through the bushes.

Of course, the other mothers were informed at once of the perversion that had been uncovered in the sumacs. None of the three mothers would believe that her boy was anything but the hapless victim of some sexual predator, so charges and counter-charges were made about who was the instigator of this crime against nature. Because he was the oldest, poor Bruno came under the most suspicion, and there were even snide remarks about his predilection for the priesthood, and of course you know about *them*.

The argument raged and spread until everyone from the West

Side was involved. Sides were taken, and for the first time cracks appeared in what Joey had always taken to be the unshakeable unity of the neighborhood. Because the families were all interrelated, the uproar was like three stones being simultaneously thrown into a pool, the ripples spreading until they overlapped, and some people found themselves with hopelessly divided loyalties. Whole families stopped speaking, and each boy was categorically forbidden to have anything to do with the others. Children unconnected with the original sin found themselves swept into the maelstrom and forbidden to consort with others who were from families known to be sympathetic or merely related to one or another of the culprits. The boys themselves were shunned by everyone. It was a lonely time, and as the summer wore on the isolation became harder and harder to bear.

One of the people with divided loyalties was Benita, a fourth cousin to Bruno, and a second cousin to both Joey and Big Paulie. Old man Fan, her father, had warned her to avoid all three boys for fear of seeming to take sides and thereby damage his position as the arbiter of neighborhood disputes. Nevertheless, several weeks after the debacle, she went looking for Joey. He was alone in the tool shed, building a scooter from a grape crate and an old pair of roller skates.

He looked up as Benita appeared in the doorway. They stared at each other in silence for a moment, then Benita said, I think this whole thing is silly, you weren't doing anything wrong.

No, Joey said, we weren't. It was just stupid.

Yes, Benita said, stupid boy stuff. You want to go to the beach with me? I think Bruno and Paulie should come too.

Joey was thunderstruck by the enormity of what she proposed to do. By appearing in public with them, she would be defying a strict neighborhood taboo and inviting ruin. He was so in awe of her quiet bravery he could barely answer. Yes, he finally said. But he wondered if he and the others would have the strength to follow her lead. Surely Bruno would.

The two of them went off to find the others. As Joey had predicted, Bruno was quick to agree. Big Paulie was reticent; it would mean disobeying the strict order of his parents to shun the company of Joey and Bruno. But when Benita employed her most potent weapon, saying, I dare you, he was unable to resist the challenge of a mere girl.

So that afternoon the four of them, Benita in the lead, followed by Joey, Bruno, and the terrified Big Paulie, trooped resolutely down the wooden stairs onto the Stevensville Beach in plain view of the entire summer community. There was a mass intake of breath and darkening of brows, but they proceeded to splash into the water and began to play as if it was the most normal day in an uneventful summer. They froze, however, as Big Paulie's mother, Serafina, stood, as did Bruno's mother, Alba, and last, Joey's mother. The three standing mothers looked at one another, then at Benita's mother, the majestic Mrs. Fantozzi, who sat impassively on her blanket. She gave no sign, but knew that a crisis, precipitated by her daughter, had been reached. Everyone held their breath, the waves themselves paused, while Mrs. Fantozzi, in the grand tradition of her family, considered her decision. After a time, she made an almost imperceptible nod to the three standing mothers. An unspoken understanding, drawn from generations of relationship extending far back into village life in the old country, passed between them. The three mothers sat back on their blankets. The four children in the water resumed their play. Gradually, the older people started to breathe again and turned back to their magazines and cigarettes. In the days that followed, people began to nod to one another when they passed, a few hesitant conversations were held about nothing in particular, children were allowed to play with one another freely, and by the coming of the warm days of August, all was as it had been.

24 AT THE BEACH

WITH THE FATHERS AWAY AND RITA TO DO THE COOKING, the mothers and children spent the weekdays in sweet indolence. As August wore on, the days got hot, and soon everyone wore bathing suits and rubber sandals from morning until sunset. After breakfast, they all waited the required hour during which Mother insisted you could not go into the water after eating for fear of getting a cramp and drowning, then took up their bags full of blankets and towels and headed for the beach.

The kids took turns carrying a cooler full of sandwiches and soda pop for the half-mile walk down Glenlord Road. The street ended on the top of a bluff overlooking the broad, sandy Stevensville beach, a well-kept secret known only to the locals and the summer residents. An old wooden staircase wound down the bluff, with benches on the landings that allowed older climbers to rest on the return journey. As they neared the end of the street, the kids dropped the cooler and ran on ahead, oblivious to the shouts of the mothers, No running!

You're going to break your necks! Bypassing the stairs, the kids ran straight down the bluff, kicking up rooster-tails of sand, until they fell, tumbling and laughing, to the bottom. They ran to reserve a good spot at the water's edge, and by the time their mothers caught up, lugging the cooler and the bags, they were already splashing in the surf, but were recalled to be slathered in suntan lotion. There were no lifeguards on the Stevensville beach, so the mothers sat on their blankets facing the water, talking, smoking, reading magazines, but always one of them, by some unspoken agreement, was watching the kids in the water.

There were only a few rules at the beach: no throwing sand, no holding anybody under, come out when your lips turn blue, and most important, no going out to the sand bar. The bottom of the beach sloped gently for some thirty feet away from shore, but then there was a sudden drop-off, then another thirty feet of deep water until the bottom rose again to a sand bar where, some sixty feet from shore, you could stand with the water at your knees at low tide. Swimming out to the sand bar was a rite of passage of even greater magnitude than riding the Parachutes and in Joey's circle had so far been accomplished only by Bruno. The younger, smaller kids were forbidden even to try because of that most dreaded beach danger, the undertow.

Undertow. The word alone was enough to strike fear into a mother's heart, and never was the water so calm that vigilance against the undertow was relaxed. The kids exploited the fear of the undertow by gradually creeping further and further out to the start of the drop-off, then bouncing up and down until their heads began to disappear, and the mothers would start yelling, Come back, you're too far out, come back right now or you'll have to get out, the undertow will get you! Joey loved to linger in the forbidden zone, his feet seeking out the cold water at the bottom, searching for a sign of the tugging at those lower depths that his mother said could suck you right out beyond help. Some day, he knew, he would defy the undertow and swim to the sand bar, perhaps the very next summer.

The waves were usually tiny at the Stevensville beach, but on occasion a storm kicked up the surf. When the waves were moderate, the kids would play in the break, skinning their arms, backs, and thighs until they were red, the coarse sand being driven deep into every bodily cavity, so that it took days for all of it to work its way out, and beds had to be emptied of sand every morning. When the waves were larger, the mothers ruled out swimming altogether and the day would be spent in various activities ashore. Smaller kids would be buried up to their necks and pictures taken. Deep holes would be dug until water was reached, then digging continued as the walls fell in, until the depression was big enough for three or four kids to inhabit, and more pictures would be taken. Sand castles were constructed, with moats that eventually caught the advancing tide and washed the castles away, and at least once a summer Father captured the destruction of a sand castle with his 8mm movie camera. Father even directed all the kids in a home movie epic called *Captain Kid's Adventure*, the title written in the sand, starring Joey and Benita as hero and heroine, and Big Paulie as the pirate villain.

When these waterside pastimes were exhausted, the kids would climb and explore the hilly dunes at the base of the bluff. It was on such a day in early August when swimming was prohibited by high surf that Joey and Benita went up into the scrubby bushes that dotted the dunes. The day was hot and the air was unusually muggy. The sky was clear and the sun baked down, but on the western horizon far out on the lake, a bank of dark storm clouds stood like a wall. Joey and Benita climbed over several small hills and found a depression on the back side of the largest dune, out of sight of both the beach and the bluff above. Here Benita decided they should dig a fort. They dug with a plastic bucket and with their hands. They sweated and their wet skin held the sand until they looked like moving nude sculptures, their bathing suits completely obscured under the coating of sand.

The wind picked up and they dug with increasing frenzy, and the hole deepened. Suddenly a great blast of wind swept in from the lake, and sand began to blow in sheets off the crest of the dune, stinging them. They huddled together in the depression they had made. The wind roared above them, and there were claps of distant thunder. Their isolation was thrilling. Joey again felt Benita's breath on his cheek, like that day in the cloak room that seemed so long ago. He looked up and found her eyes looking into his. Joey made a tiny move in Benita's direction. Benita answered with a tiny move toward Joey. In a series of halting increments, they brought their lips together, gently because of the sand. They held them there. The outside world receded and grew silent. Joey felt himself falling into Benita, deeper and deeper. Then their isolation exploded as a tremndous clap of thunder shook the dune.

The roar of the wind was deafening as they peeked over the crest of the dune, squinting against the blowing sand. Spread out below them was a scene that looked like the end of the world. Looming high into the sky was the black wall of storm clouds, now much closer and advancing rapidly, illuminated from within by flashes of lightning, the rolling thunder almost continuous. In the water, a few swimmers were frantically splashing toward shore, the huge waves whipped into white foam. A sheet of lightning swept the water beyond the sand bar. On the beach, people were running, trying to catch runaway blankets, towels, and beach umbrellas. Their mothers were running toward them, waving their arms frantically, their mouths working but their voices lost under the storm. Joey and Benita crested the hill and ran into the teeth of the wind until they reached their mothers, who yelled, Where have you been, we've been looking all over, you scared us to death, a boy was caught in the undertow.

Joey and Benita looked toward the water. A knot of people struggled out of the surf carrying a body. They brought it up on the beach and laid it down. Joey broke from his mother's grasp and ran forward, seized with a terrible premonition. Mother ran after him, yelling, No, don't go there, you can't help. But Joey ran on until he reached the circle of people looking down.

The boy was face down in the sand. A man straddled him and began to press his back, rhythmically, one, two, one, two. Joey dropped to the sand and looked between the legs of the crowd, but he couldn't see the boy's face. Benita was suddenly beside him. People in the crowd were yelling to one another over the storm, saying, The storm kicked up the undertow, he was too far out, maybe the lightning got him, somebody went for the firemen, they'll never get here in time. A cold rain began to fall, washing the caked sand off Joey and Benita.

Then Bruno's mother, Alba, wailing, broke through the circle, threw herself on her knees, and lifted Bruno's head in her hands. Joey screamed but no sound came out. Benita fell to the sand and started to sob. The man kept pushing on Bruno's back, one, two, one, two. Alba looked up at the crowd and cried, *Preghi con me, preghi con me*! Pray with me, pray with me! Everyone sank to their knees. All up and down the beach, people saw them, and they too knelt beside the roaring surf as the lightning danced overhead and the thunder rolled along the coast. They lowered their heads and prayed, dozens of them in the cold rain, prayed while Alba screamed, but Joey could not pray, not to a God who had allowed this to happen.

Finally the man pumping Bruno's body slowed and stopped, then got up and turned away and wept, and everyone turned away and wept except Joey, who knelt beside Alba and reached out his hand and touched Bruno's matted hair, and remembered the day in the tunnel under the backyard and the many times Bruno had protected him and most of all, the trip to the block party and the secret that Bruno had entrusted him with that day on the El. But now there would be no Father Bruno, no changing people's hearts, no changing the world. Joey was cold as ice clear through, his eyes empty. He knew at that moment, finally and completely, that life was not what he had imagined, that no one was safe, not ever, and that even the joy of a kiss would be forever tinged with mortality.

25 GOODBYE

THE DAY AFTER BRUNO'S DEATH, the caravan of neighborhood cars formed and they all drove back to the West Side. In every car there was silence broken only by occasional murmurs of dismay and comfort. Two days later, Joey found himself again in the main parlor of Leo Anzilotti's Funeral Home, and again Father Louis came and led a novena, this time alone, and this time Joey and Benita knelt together and joined the quiet prayers. Over and over Father Louis intoned, Our Father Who art in Heaven, and the murmured response from the assembled mourners flowed over the room like a pedal tone from an organ. Joey's lips formed the words of the prayers without meaning, bringing no light into the dark void that filled him. All that day and night, and all the next day, the prayers continued and still Benita was at his side, as unfelt by Joey as the cold and hard and endless rosary beads that slipped one by one through his fingers.

That night, it was time to say goodbye. Joey and Benita came forward. Bruno looked as Nonno had looked, asleep and waxy, like a statue of himself. Joey bent and kissed Bruno's cheek. Then he watched, oddly unmoved, as Bruno's mother said her goodbye and the lid of the casket was lowered on his boyhood.

After the Solemn High Funeral Mass the next day, Joey was one of the pallbearers who carried Bruno's coffin out of St. Michael the Archangel's church. He looked down as he held the brass handle and saw in the gleaming casket the reflection of a face he didn't recognize. At the Queen of Heaven mausoleum, Bruno was swallowed whole by the dark hole in the marble wall and took his place in that silent city. This time Joey didn't find it barbaric, nor frightening; he didn't feel anything, nor did he dream that night.

That Friday everyone except Bruno's folks drove back to Stevensville. It didn't occur to anyone to stop at the Dairy Maid.

The few remaining weeks of summer passed gently, one day merging into another. The summer storms came and went. The steam trains were no longer noticed as they thundered past. The leaves of the grapevines began to turn golden and there was talk of the harvest that would come too late for any of the Chicagoans to see. The nights grew prematurely cold, and for the first time Joey saw a fire in Harvey Seasongood's potbelly stove. Most days, Joey sat alone in his secret place, watching the creek slow to a trickle, then become merely a dark stain running through the grass.

Late one afternoon, as the end of summer vacation approached, he was lying on the grass beside the creek, looking up at the clouds, imagining shapes in them, thinking about nothing and everything, when Benita appeared, looking down at him. Here you are, she said, I've missed you.

How did you find me?

I saw you come in here once, and it wasn't hard to follow the path. I hope you don't mind.

Joey sat up and said, No, no, I don't mind at all, I'm glad.

Benita sat beside him and looked around and said, This is a nice place, I can see why you like it.

They sat in silence for a time. Then Benita said, I heard that you're going to move.

Joey nodded. He said softly, My folks found a house they want to buy.

There was more silence, then Benita asked, Is it far away?

No, Joey said, it's just out by the Zoo, in Brookfield, near where my Nonno Lorenzo lived.

Benita nodded, That's a nice place, lots of trees.

More silence.

Benita sighed. Then she said simply, I miss Bruno.

Yes, me too.

Benita thought for a while, then said, It changes things.

Yes, it does.

She reached out and took his hand. They sat there a long time.

Then Joey said, You could come to visit when you go to the Zoo.

Benita nodded, and said, and you'll be coming back to the West Side sometimes, I'll see you then.

Sure, Joey said.

JOEY AND HIS FAMILY MOVED A WEEK BEFORE SCHOOL WAS TO START. On what would be his last day on the West Side, Joey got up early and went to the coffee shop, waiting for Booker T to come with the rack and bottles that would now permanently belong to him. Joey stood outside, watching the streetcars pass. By half past eight, Booker T had not arrived and Joey went inside.

The fat woman with frizzy hair was still behind the counter, and the same large man was sitting on his stool. They turned and looked at Joey when he came in. The woman greeted him warmly, Hi, haven't seen you all summer.

Joey said, I was in Michigan, and now we're going to move to Brookfield.

My, my, the woman said, won't that be nice!

The man looked up from his coffee and said, Hell, you can go to the Zoo anytime you want.

Yes, Joey said. But I was wondering about a boy from the factory. He was going to get the coffee while I was gone. I thought I'd meet him here, but he hasn't come.

The man at the counter snorted and said, Little picaninny, was he?

The word hit Joey like a fist. He swallowed the thing that rose in his throat and said only, He was colored, yes, have you seen him?

The woman drew herself up and said, He came in here one day with your bottles and all, and I thought maybe he had stole them from you, so I called the police.

Joey felt his heart sink. No, he said, I gave him the bottles and rack. He was taking over the coffee run for me.

Well, the woman said, that's what he said, but we didn't believe him.

Hell, the man grunted, it don't matter, the police didn't do nuthin', just run him off. Never do nuthin', what do we pay taxes for?

The woman busied herself wiping the counter and said, Anyways, we don't serve no niggers in here, so I ain't seen him since.

Joey's stomach was in a knot, his jaw and fists clenched, his breath caught in his throat. He looked at the woman who had given him so many doughnuts, who had encouraged him, and whose own dreams had evaporated in the clouds of steam that rose from the coffee urns. She bent over the counter, wiping hard. A cold fury rose slowly from the pit of Joey's stomach, filled his chest, and overflowed into his mouth like bile. Through clenched teeth he said, Shame on you.

The woman spun around, startled, and stared at him, her mouth open as if to reply, but no sound came out. Joey stared at her and the man, his eyes burning. His voice hissed, Shame, shame on you all! You just go to hell, both of you! Then he turned and ran out, stunned silence in his wake.

Joey ran all the way up Western to Cermak and into the dark and silent alley behind the factory. He stopped and saw that there was no steam coming from the vents. Even the garbage cans were empty. He went to the window and tried to look in. He knocked and listened for a response, but heard nothing. He pushed against the window and it opened. He called inside, Hello! Booker T? Luther? Anyone? There was only the echo of his own voice. He pulled himself up on the bars and looked in. There was no one there, the vats were empty and cold, there were no shiny parts hanging from the chains. He yelled again.

Somewhere a door opened and there was a shuffling in the darkness. The old black security guard came to the window and said gruffly, What you want, boy?

Joey said, I used to bring coffee to the workers here, and I'm leaving the neighborhood and I wanted to say goodbye.

The old guard shook his head and said, They all gone, factory's closed.

Joey said, There was a man named Luther, and a boy, about my age, named Booker T.

Shit, the guard said, there was lots of them. They all gone now, whoever they was, and you better go too.

And he shut the window and latched it from the inside.

Joey stood for a time, feeling a great emptiness, a great stillness, then wandered out of the alley and past the empty schoolyard without seeing it. He thought he might go and find Bruno to ask what he should do, but in the next moment remembered that he could never do that again. He wandered across the street, past the corner where he had helped Benita through the snow so long ago, and up Oakley Avenue. As he passed the mouth of his alley, the Regsaliar came past, singing his song, his horse clopping and his ancient wagon groaning. Joey looked up at him, and the old black man with the white beard nodded gravely and went on singing.

On Twenty-Second Place, another day was beginning. The horse-drawn produce wagon was moving down the street, the driver ringing his bell and calling *frutta e vegetali, frutta e vegetali,* the women coming down their steps. Around the corner at the other end of the street, the man who sharpened knives and scissors came calling, *coltelli e forbici, coltelli e forbici,* pushing his handcart with the gong that made the haunting ding-dong.

Joey listened to their calls and bells, the clopping of the horses, the distant song of the Regsaliar, and knew in that instant that it was the music of a passing world, so beautiful it hurt, and that it would soon fall silent forever.

ALL THE REST OF THAT WEEK THE FAMILY FINISHED ITS PACKING, and Father and some friends brought the big rented truck and filled it with their furniture and boxes of belongings. Big Paulie and Peter came over to help, and Joey said his goodbyes to them. When everything was packed, Joey went for a last walk down the street that had been his world for his first ten years on earth. At the corner of Oakley Avenue, he stopped in front of Benita's fancy yellow pressed-brick house. He opened the gate and walked up the steps. He was about to push the doorbell button, but tears began to force themselves from his eyes for the first time since that day on the beach, and his throat tightened so he could scarcely breathe. He turned away and ran.

Early the next morning they pulled away, waving to Nonna Augusta and Nonno Beppino, who seemed genuinely aggrieved by their leaving. Father drove the moving truck and Mother and Joey followed in Bedelia, both of them in the front seat, the back seat filled with plants and other things too delicate to be put in the truck. They moved slowly down Twenty-Second Place toward Oakley Avenue. Big Paulie and some others waved from their porches. Bruno's house stood dark and cold and silent.

As they rounded the corner, Joey saw Benita looking out the front window of the yellow pressed-brick house. She watched him pass. He waved, and she lifted one hand and pressed it gently against the glass. She stayed like that, perfectly still. Joey pressed his hand against the window of the car, and held it there until she was out of sight.

Even in the blur of moving into their new house, meeting new neighbors, exploring the mysteries of a new neighborhood, the image of Benita at the window remained vivid in Joey's mind for days, but slowly faded and became indistinct.

Joey's tenth year drew to a close. He went to a new school and was put back a grade, so he was no longer the youngest. He made new friends his own age. After a time, the old neighborhood seemed further and further away, in another time, another world. He heard news of Benita from his mother and once even spoke to her on the phone, but never saw her again, just as he never again saw Peter, Big

Paulie, or the malevolent Rex, and never discovered the fate of Walter Siroka. As the years passed, Riverview was torn down, and the huge family gatherings at Easter, Thanksgiving, and Christmas grew smaller and smaller as, one after another, his aunts, uncles, and cousins moved away and his remaining grandparents died. Fontana's closed, and Leo Anzilotti became his own last customer. People stopped going to Stevensville for the summer and Rita's Resort, the Starlight Drive-in, the House of David, and Harvey Seasongood's Emporium and Scale all drifted into memory, though for the rest of his life a chance sound, like the ding-dong of a distant ice cream truck, or the smell of baking bread, or a glimpse of a vaguely familiar face, would summon them for a few moments. The music-filled house on Drexel Avenue, Luther touching his heart, and Booker T staring out through the rusty iron bars were the last images to fade.

Bruno's understanding smile never quite entirely left him.

Eventually, Joey married and his own family grew and made their way to other cities, and by the time his parents died he was on the other side of the continent from them, far away from the West Side, far away in every way except those that mattered most.

The Long Italian Goodbye

Robert Benedetti

A READER'S GUIDE AND DISCUSSION GROUP TOPICS

A Look Back at the Heart of Italy

by Robert Benedetti

IN 2004, MY WIFE OF THIRTY-EIGHT YEARS finally persuaded me to take her back to the old neighborhood. She and my children had listened patiently for years to the stories that I and my family told of life on Chicago's West Side, some of which – but not all – are included in *The Long Italian Goodbye*. So when visiting my best and oldest friend who now owns a restaurant called *The Chef's Station* in Evanston, we took a day to drive to the old neighborhood, which the magazines and websites now grandly call *The Heart of Italy*.

Surprisingly, Oakley Avenue and Twenty-Second Place looked much the same on the sunny winter afternoon when we pulled off Cermak, but there were important differences. There were more cars parked everywhere, fewer trees, and, most noticeably, no people at all. The street was silent and still, like a photograph, and seemed to me to have a feeling of isolation. Perhaps it was the aluminum storm doors and windows that now covered many of the porches which, in Joey's day, had been open and unprotected. But I could not remember a time when the old neighborhood had been so devoid of life.

After some minutes, a man came out of a house and approached his car. He happily answered our questions about the inhabitants, but most of the names he mentioned were unfamiliar and most were non-Italian. He knew little about his neighbors who, in Joey's time, would have been extended family members, their most intimate secrets part of village lore.

As I walked the route through the gangway between the houses and through the backyard that I, like Joey, had taken to school every morning, I saw that many more of the rear porches were enclosed, as ours had been, and most were sided with asphalt shingles. The alley had finally been paved, and the empty lot built up. Across the street, Pickard School sported a new brick addition, only a glimpse of the old building peeking out from one side.

We walked south on Oakley Avenue, the way Joey and I had gone to go to church at Saint Michael's, and to get bread and milk. Fontana's Bakery was boarded up, though the stone cornice on the building still bore the name FONTANA BROS. But the cooperative market across the street was still there, now Miceli's Deli, and on this end of Oakley there was a feeling of vitality and signs of gentrification. Decorated stone seating places were placed along the sidewalk and there were several fashionable new restaurants that have sprung up in place of the venerable Toscano's (where Joey's father had been a waiter) like Ignotz, Bacchanalia, Fontanella's, and Martin's Bar. Food, we were glad to see, was still at the heart of the old neighborhood, and we promised ourselves to return some day for the annual Taste of Italy Festival held on Oakley on Father's Day weekend.

We passed the new restaurants by, however, because Bella Bruna's restaurant was open for lunch, still hale and hearty since its opening in 1933. Inside we found Bella's picture (as a much older woman) smiling down on the dining room, its walls still adorned by murals. A new family owns and operates the restaurant now, but knows and values its history.

As we came out, we were confronted by Anzilotti's Funeral Home, still there, stone façade still regal, a solid, dignified presence. Perhaps it was because I had recently turned sixty-five, but it looked to me like it was waiting.

Sitting in front of Anzilotti's on one of the benches, like a specter from the past, was a very old woman dressed just as she would have been in 1948. A few questions in my halting Italian revealed that she had indeed known my grandmothers and their sisters, though not my parents. Her wizened face awoke in me a dim glimmer of memory, but it would not come into focus.

Around the corner, St. Michael's sported a new school, though the church – looking impossibly small now – was locked, as it never would have been in Joey's day.

That locked door was, for me, the perfect metaphor of our visit.

Thankfully, I had said my goodbyes by writing this book, and as much as I miss it, I understand now that we can none of us go back to our villages.

You who are lucky enough to live in neighborhoods like Joey's – and I know there are still some left today – must give deep thanks and fight to keep them alive. As Woody Guthrie once said, the future of our country "depends on people who are willing to stay in one place and put down roots." For the rest of us, let us cherish our families and keep our heritage alive as best we can.

★ ★ ★

A website devoted to the Italian neighborhoods of Chicago can be found at http://littleitalychicago.com. It contains links to information on Joey's neighborhood, The Heart of Italy, including an excellent factual history by John Insalata.

Reading Group Questions and Topics for Discussion

1. The "old country" was an important part of Joey's life and the life of his neighborhood, which was in many ways a village transplanted whole from Tuscany. For Italians and non-Italians alike, what is the importance of the traditions brought from the old country by our many immigrant peoples?

2. How does language relate to these traditions? How important is it to keep the old language alive?

3. The kitchen was the heart of the home for Joey and his family, and on any day the Nonnas of the neighborhood could be found there. Today's resurgence of interest in Italian cooking is part of a larger desire to revive tradition, but there are few three-generation homes left with women (and sometimes men) available to cook and shop on a daily basis the way our grandmothers did. How do we compensate for this? Is there a way to keep the home fires burning, literally, and in the hearts of our young people?

4. Are there neighborhoods like Joey's today? What pressures are causing them to disappear? What might be done to preserve them?

5. How important to our well-being as individuals is the sense of belonging to a tradition? How important is a sense of ethnic tradition to our families?

6. How can we foster a sense of local history and tradition in our young people?

7. The church and its festivals was important to Joey's neighborhood. How do our religious institutions function as repositories of local tradition within neighborhoods today?

8. Consider Joey's experience of racial discrimination and his reaction to it. Did you have similar experiences?

9. Did reading about Joey's neighborhood elicit memories of the neighborhood in which you grew up? If so, share them with your friends, and most importantly, with your family.

10. Our culture was at one time called a "melting pot." As ethnic groups began to struggle to retain their cultural identities, the label "salad bowl" began to replace "melting pot" to signify the possibility of retaining a positive diversity within our culture. Sadly, the events of 9/11 and the War on Terror have made questions of ethnic diversity and immigration even more difficult and pressing. Consider what the decline of ethnic traditions like those in Joey's neighborhood means for our country, and how we can reconcile them to current conditions.

ABOUT THE AUTHOR

A multiple Emmy and Peabody Award-winning film producer and distinguished teacher of acting and directing, Robert Benedetti received his PhD from Northwestern University. He was an early member of Chicago's Second City Theatre, then taught acting for over thirty years. He was Chairman of Theatre at York University in Toronto, Head of the Acting Program at the Yale Drama School, and Dean of Theatre at The California Institute of the Arts. He is currently on the faculty at the University of Nevada, Las Vegas. He has directed at many regional theatres and festivals. As President of Ted Danson's Anasazi Productions at Paramount Studios, he won Emmys for producing the films *MISS EVERS' BOYS* and *A LESSON BEFORE DYING* for HBO. Benedetti has written six books on acting and film production. In 2005 he received the Lifetime Career Achievement Award from the Association for Theatre in Higher Education. *The Long Italian Goodbye* is his first novel. He and his wife live in Santa Monica, California. He can be reached at www.robertbenedetti.com.

Watch for the next Joey novel, due in 2006. It will follow Joey into the fifties and the adventures and perils of high school and girls.

And don't miss Robert Benedetti's second novel,

An Affair of State
A Gourmet Mystery in Eight Courses

Coming from Durban House soon! A tale of murder, revolution, and political intrigue, it is set at a banquet on the Island of Cyprus on the eve of World War I. For an exciting preview, please turn the page...

First Course: Oysters Lucifer

"CANNOT BE USUAL PRICE!" The old fisherman, stinking of sweat and fish, was yelling, his face red, the veins in his neck bulging. It was a well-rehearsed and effective performance. Some of the other fishermen on the dock paused to watch him in admiration. He took a deep breath. "Is holiday, must be more!"

Nicephorous Phocos, called simply Nicky by everyone, wanted to applaud. Instead he put on a stern face and offered a bonus of fifty drachmas. The wily old man, his face sun-darkened and wrinkled, only shook his head. "Double!" he said. Nicky didn't have time to argue. He opened the large wallet marked with the royal coat-of-arms chained to his belt and counted three hundred drachmas into the man's leathery hand, pockmarked with old hook scars. The fisherman smiled, showing the few teeth left in his mouth, and gestured toward the crates of oysters, still dripping, on the dock.

With the help of the fisherman, Nicky hefted the oysters up into the back of the embassy truck. Though it was not yet seven, the heat was beginning to build, and Nicky knew that as he drove away from the coast the heat would rise even faster. During the two hours it would take him to drive to Nicosia – and that at emergency speed and barring delays – the oysters would be in grave danger of spoiling. So Nicky gave the old man another fifty drachmas, and together they provisioned the truck with straw bales, in which the oysters were packed with precious ice – for another hundred drachmas! Nicky hoped that Governor Woodford, who had insisted that the *hors-d'oeurves* include several oyster dishes, could justify this outrageous expense on the embassy's accounts. But then, that was not Nicky's problem; his job at present was to get the oysters back safely.

Nicky climbed behind the wheel, flicking a Roman salute at the old man, who cackled. As he pulled away, Nicky couldn't help smiling. The old fox! He knew Nicky had to have the oysters and that these were the last available on this Saint's Day, when the other more devout fishermen of Kyrenia – which the Turks called Girne – refused to sail. Like any of the Greek Cypriots, the old man took special delight in charging the British embassy an exorbitant rate, and though Nicky had to make a show of outrage at the price, in his heart he was glad to see the British money in the hands of his countryman.

Kyrenia, the port closest to the capital city of Nicosia, was a bustling place on most days, but on this sacred feast day it was reflectively quiet. Winding his way up the bumpy, cobbled street that led south, Nicky had to wait for a procession of angelic children, all in white, singing as they followed a statue of Saint Barnabas through the narrow streets toward the Greek Orthodox church that bore his name. For a moment Nicky was transported to that sultry day twenty years past but still fresh in his mind, when he had followed a statue of a different saint in his own town, his family standing proudly alongside the foot-worn street, his mother smiling and waving, his father looming proudly behind her, the smells of the street vendors' offerings making his mouth water in anticipation of the feast that his grandmother and aunts were laying out at the family's farm, the culmination of three days of steady kitchen labor. Would they ever come again, he wondered, such carefree, golden days – either for him or for his country?

Over the children's song, Nicky could hear the church bells ringing. High on the hill above the docks loomed the enormous medieval Kyrenia Castle, while in its shadow the masts of the fishing boats waved slowly as if in homage to the saint, and the brilliant Mediterranean sun sparkled on the green waters of the harbor. Nicky took a deep breath, feeling blessed to have been born on such a glorious island as Cyprus, but simultaneously and equally aggrieved that the island was still, as it had been for centuries, under the yoke of yet another foreign power, the very power from which he made a good living, enough to support his widowed mother and aunts. The old conflict between his dependency on the embassy and his yearning to see this glorious island free sat in his gut like a piece of undigested fish, and gave the sparkle of the blue waters and the slow waving of the masts in the harbor a twinge of melancholy.

Makarios, the imperious chef of the embassy, had insisted that the oysters be as fresh as possible. It was at best a two-hour drive to Nicosia (which Nicky privately called by its local name, Lefkosia), but Nicky was determined to make record time. The truck bounced violently over the rutted roads and the engine howled in complaint as the truck swung and wove, raising clouds of dust at every hairpin turn as it wound its way up into the foothills of the Kyrenia Mountains, which stretched away to the west, rising to the distant summit of Mount Olimbos, while to the east the brown, parched fields stretched to the sea.

The windscreen was caked with dust and Nicky turned on the wipers, just in time to avoid hitting a shepherd in a wide straw hat who was leading his flock across the road. The roadway was filled by the animals and Nicky slowly forced his way through, honking furiously and nudging more than one of the wooly bundles out of his way. These domestic sheep were much whiter and better-kept than the brown-haired wild sheep, the *moufflon*, who roamed higher in the forests. The shepherd waved his staff and shouted angrily, and his dog barked and snapped at the truck tires.

The road grew rougher as he moved higher toward the pass that led to Nicosia. This northern district of the island was dotted with mines. Some were ancient, abandoned copper mines – the name Cyprus came from *Kipros*, the Greek word for copper – and they dated from the Greek civilization that had thrived here in 1200 B.C. For centuries, the island had been a Greek kingdom, and during that golden age had produced the thousands of precious statues and other antiquities that now were unearthed almost daily in the busy archeological sites intermingled among the mines. Surely, Nicky thought, no other piece of earth has been so poked and prodded, so honeycombed with holes.

And yet it retained its beauty, even against the more recent strip mines built by the British to dig asbestos and the many other minerals with which the island was blessed – or cursed, Nicky thought, since they had made the "Island of Dreams" an attractive target for an endless succession of foreign rulers. Cyprus, he knew, had an unequaled history of foreign domination stretching back over three thousand years to the sad time when those first Greek settlers were supplanted by a succession of invaders, from the ancient Assyrians, Moroccans, Persians, and Romans, to the more recent French, Venetians, and, since 1571, the hated Turks.

And then, forty years ago, the Turks, while keeping possession, had allowed the British to build a naval base at Akrotiri and to administer the island, in return for protecting Turkish lands and payment of a small annual tribute. How like the Turks, Nicky thought, to borrow a navy ready-made and so easily to sacrifice Cyprus as payment. The thought that the British were probably the best of the bad lot of foreign rulers did little to soften his bitterness that in all the thousands of years since those glorious ancient days, Greece had never once ruled the island again.

As the truck crested the pass, a blessedly cool breeze stirred the trees and Nicky allowed himself the luxury of slowing and leaning out the window to breathe deeply and wipe the sweat from his neck and forehead. He looked to the west and was gladdened, as always, by the full glory of Mount Olimbos rising up in the distance. It was named in homage to Olympus, of course, but the name had been changed sufficiently to maintain a respectful deference to the Greek original.

Nicky felt as blessed to live on the flanks of Olimbos as he would to live near the sacred mountain's Grecian namesake. It was in a meadow halfway up the mountain where, as a school boy, he had lost his virginity. It was, in fact, that same meadow to which he had taken Lydia only three days ago. It hadn't been a conscious choice; he had realized the coincidence only after they had arrived. But now he wondered whether his feelings for Lydia didn't unconsciously represent a new passage in his life, as if the loss of his physical virginity ten years ago was now, at age 27, followed by a loss of emotional virginity, a surrender to feelings that were unfamiliar and frightening. He had never experienced a passion as strong except his passion for liberty, and the collision of these two passions filled him with a deep foreboding.

He downshifted and continued over the pass. The warm summer air and the rocking of the truck on the rutted mountain road almost lulled Nicky into a doze as he descended out of the mountains and into the rolling foothills, carpeted with fruit orchards. Some of the citrus trees were still in bloom, and the scent was so heavy in the air Nicky could taste it.

Lower down, he emerged into the broad plain of Mesaoria, with its endless fields of wheat waving like an ocean in the summer breeze. Nicky had been born near here, on his family's farm, and in the distance he could see the spire of his village above the wheat. As it always did, the sight filled him with bittersweet memories of those innocent childhood days and the simple pleasures and pains of rural life. How he longed to return to that quiet existence, but life had set him on another, potentially violent path.

Nicky shook himself out of his reverie as he neared Nicosia. The clusters of homes on the outskirts of the city began to displace the farmland, and Nicky was fully alert by the time he guided the truck through the narrow northern gate that pierced the thick, ancient walls around the oldest section of the city, some five kilometers across. Nicky guided the truck expertly through the maze of narrow streets, rumbled over the ancient bridge that spanned the Pedieos River, and entered the broad central plaza before which stood the majestic fourteenth-century Cathedral of Saint Sophia. Horn blaring, the truck wove slowly through the pushcarts and vendors' stalls of the perpetual market that was clustered around the cathedral. On the broad steps of the cathedral, he saw Father Demetrius.

Father Demetrius saw the embassy truck bouncing into the plaza and recognized Nicky behind the wheel. As the truck passed, he made a diminutive Sign of the Cross in Nicky's direction, a silent benediction. Nicky nodded as their eyes met.

Father Demetrius was not a native Cypriot. He had been born in Athens in a squalid slum on the flanks of the Acropolis, and had taken refuge in the church at an early age. Under the doting patronage of a venerable old priest, he had entered instruction as an acolyte when he was still a teenager. Before he had been ordained, however, he had suffered a crisis of faith that for a time drove him out of the seminary. He had entered the secular world with a vengeance, devouring its pleasures like a starving man at a banquet. After a year of frenetic debauchery, he landed in a paupers' hospital with gonorrhea, cirrhosis of the liver, a severe kidney infection, and the beginnings of consumption. As he hung between life and death, he promised God that if he lived he would renew his faith and devote his life to the work of the church. Nursed back to health by a gruff old nun, he had kept his promise. After his ordination, he was assigned to a remote rural parish on Cyprus, but his extraordinary energy and steely determination had quickly come to the notice of his bishop, and he was soon named to the staff of Saint Sophia's Cathedral. He threw himself completely into the life of his parish and soon, in the way of all converts, became more Cypriot than the Cypriots.

Like the other islanders, Father Demetrius had at first welcomed the British. Emissaries of the British government had publicly espoused the ideal of self-governance for the island. To the vast majority of islanders, self-governance meant *enosis – union* – with Greece, and a return to the founding culture of the island. They had hoped that the British would use their influence with the Turks to bring this long-delayed dream to fruition, but gradually it became clear that Britain, like every other foreign oppressor, was interested only in what it could get from the island: asbestos and other minerals, antique works of art for their museums, and most of all a prime military base in the Mediterranean.

As his disappointment with the British betrayal of the promised independence grew, Father Demetrius first joined, then came to lead the *enosis* movement. He was its spiritual mainspring, and to his own surprise, he soon found himself encouraging his otherwise complacent flock to open rebellion. Under the uplifted and indifferent noses of the British authorities, he had secretly built a substantial guerilla force that now numbered some thousand committed members. Nicky, because of his strong position within the embassy, was one of the earliest and most important conscripts.

And now, the tribute festival had become a rallying point for the movement. This annual two-day festival, beginning with a great banquet and climaxing at noon the following day with the ceremony in which Britain paid its yearly tribute to the Turkish sultan for control of the island, had become the symbolic focus for their simmering rage, an emblem of the way their blessed island was used as a mere pawn by others. The festival, when diplomats from all over Europe would be assembled on the island, had to be used for some sort of dramatic demonstration that would alert the world to their plight. Father Demetrius prayed for inspiration.

★ ★ ★

FRAULEIN BURSTNER GRIPPED THE HANDRAILS as the ship lurched. Three years ago she had taken this same voyage to cover the installation of that prig Woodford, the new British governor of Cyprus. Afraid of a repetition of the seasickness she had suffered then, she had asked her Aunt Greta, the seasoned world traveler, for advice. Greta had said that she should avoid eating on the day of the voyage, stay on deck, breathe deeply, and fix her eyes on the horizon. She had done all that, but with every roll and pitch of the ship she felt her stomach churn and her mouth fill with bile. Damn! She remembered Greta's joke: There were two stages of seasickness, the first in which you were afraid you were going to die, and the second in which you were afraid you weren't. The joke didn't seem funny now, as she was just passing from the first stage to the second. She began to understand the stories of seasick sailors who had tied themselves to the mast in order to avoid throwing themselves overboard.

Nevertheless, it was not so much the seasickness itself, though that was terrible enough, but the indignity of it that angered her. Hildegard Burstner, famous correspondent for *Der Geist*, the most widely-read foreign correspondent in Germany, who had covered wars, floods, famines, and just one month ago the assassination of the Archduke Ferdinand, whose dispatches were translated and syndicated all across Europe, was not someone who should be clutching miserably at the rail above a surging sea, retching like a common tourist.

She had managed to travel overland almost the whole way from Germany, except for the brief and placid ferry across the Strait of Bosporus, and had sought out the shortest possible water route to the island. Even so, the ferry from Alanya to Cyprus, a distance of only some ninety kilometers, took five hours, only one of which remained to be suffered. She tried to distract herself from her present misery by thinking about her assignment. She had undertaken more dangerous assignments in the past, of course, but the urgency of the situation and the enormity of the possible consequences made this one very special. Certainly she would have suffered a sea voyage, even one as short as this, for nothing less.

And, of course, for the chance to see Olga again.

★ ★ ★

NICKY SHIFTED INTO THE LOWEST GEAR and the truck complained as it labored up the winding road that led to the embassy, a massive stone pile in the manner of English baronial estates, that sat atop the highest hill in the city like a Parthenon on its own Acropolis. At last, in a shower of gravel, it skidded to a stop at the kitchen's loading dock just as the embassy clock was striking ten. Nicky honked the horn urgently. A crew of kitchen helpers rushed out and hauled the crate up the back stairs and into the pandemonium of the kitchen.

Cooks were rushing to prepare the elaborate banquet Governor Woodford had ordered over the objections of Makarios, the beleaguered chef, who even now was yelling orders to his sous-chef, cooks, and helpers. He turned as Nicky came in. "Did you get them?" he asked.

"Yes," Nicky panted, "the only load in port, fresh from the sea."

"Thank God," Makarios said, crossing himself, "another half hour and it would have been too late." He ordered several kitchen boys to get busy shucking the oysters as the poaching pans were readied. "The devil take Woodford and his dinner," Makarios muttered. "Saint Barnabas himself could not have endured it!"

Brochettes d'Huîtres Lucifer – Skewers of Oysters Lucifer
Poach some fine oysters, bearded, in their own liquor; dry them, and dip them into thin mustard. Skewer them, six at a time, on skewers. Dip them in a mixture of well-beaten eggs, salt, pepper, and one teaspoon oil per egg. Next roll them in flour, and then in fine bread crumbs. Fry them at the last moment, and serve them on a napkin.

Makarios turned to check the seasoning of the consommé in the huge stockpot beside the main stove. The burly cook was a distant cousin of Nicky's and had grown up not far from the embassy in one of the poorer sections of the city. Nicky understood that Makarios' motives in joining the *enosis* underground were very different from his own. While Nicky was inspired by a love of the land itself and the desire to reconnect with the island's classical past, Makarios and some others were driven by resentment for the comparative poverty in which most of the native islanders had been kept by their various foreign oppressors despite the vast riches those oppressors extracted from the island and so ostentatiously displayed. When the embassy itself was built by the sweat of Cypriot labor, and filled to overflowing with priceless Cypriot antiquities, the British had by their mindless arrogance insulted and inflamed the natives, whom they considered to be no more threatening than a flock of sheep, fit only to be herded and shorn.

Watching the chef stirring his soup, the muscles of his back rippling under his tunic, Nicky thought that he and Makarios were the two aspects of the *enosis* movement — he cerebral and cautious by nature, Makarios muscular and impulsive. They had tremendous power as long as they worked in consort. But should they fall into disharmony... Nicky shrugged the thought away.

Makarios held out a spoonful of soup to Nicky and asked, "What do you think?"

Nicky blew across the soup to cool it, then sucked it in. "A little more salt."

"Thirteen dishes in eight courses!" Makarios cursed as he sprinkled sea salt into the soup. "The governor says such extravagance is the minimum at state affairs in England and France, where more than twenty courses are often served. I tell him that Cyprus isn't England. He says the embassy is British soil and we must serve as they would in London! It's insane!"

In fact, Nicky himself had argued that a simple dinner of native dishes would be considered quaint and interesting by the foreign guests, but Governor Alfred Woodford, OBE, had insisted on a traditional banquet in the grand manner, which was to say, in the tradition of the great Parisian chef, Escoffier. To make matters worse, Woodford had insisted on selecting certain dishes in honor of various guests, with several courses dedicated to a certain Russian actress with whom, rumor had it, Woodford had once been intimate.

Makarios muttered again, "Insane!"

Nicky patted the sweating chef on the shoulder. "His time here will soon end. Might as well give him what he wants."

★ ★ ★

ERNST STREISEL, the most accomplished covert agent in the Austrian Secret Police, was a man both revered and feared by his superiors. Revered because he had managed to infiltrate the dreaded Black Hand, spending several years undercover in what was one of the most secretive and dangerous organizations in Europe, and feared because his methods were radical and unpredictable. He was, in fact, so loose a cannon that Gruber, his immediate superior, had several times considered terminating him, fearful that Streisel had "gone native," as the British sometimes put it.

But each time Streisel had proven his value. Gruber had been forced to admit that the man, while ungovernable, was indispensable. When, only two days before the assassination of the Archduke Ferdinand, Streisel had brought word of the plot, Gruber found the idea so outlandish that he had hesitated to act on it. Streisel's suspicions were, after all, based merely on the mailing of a single scrap of a newspaper article announcing the impending visit of the Archduke Ferdinand to Sarajevo. But Streisel insisted that because of the identity of the sender, and those to whom it was sent, it could only be interpreted as a signal for the plot to come to fruition.

Gruber had finally been persuaded to take Streisel's information to the Austrian Foreign Minister, Count Berchtold. Unlike Gruber, the count was immediately inclined to accept the validity of Streisel's interpretation. But to Gruber's surprise, Berchtold ordered him to do nothing.

It was only after the assassination itself the following day that Gruber realized the brilliance of Berchtold's decision. By refusing to prevent the murder of Ferdinand, Berchtold had given Austria an excuse for invasion of Serbia that was far more valuable to the Austrian war party than its much-disliked leader, the Archduke, had ever been.

And now, with the invasion imminent, Gruber had given Streisel the most critical assignment of his career: to rush with all haste to Cyprus, there to receive a secret document that would be crucial to their plans for war with Serbia. In it was the truth about the rumored treaty between Italy, Britain, France, and Russia, a treaty that could prove disastrous to the Austrian cause. Streisel was to verify the contents and send them his report by the new encrypted radio installed aboard the A65, the fastest patrol boat in the Austrian fleet, stationed at their secret base at Dubrovnik.

Immediately, Streisel activated his contacts on Cyprus, and that very night was underway in the Adriatic at flank speed. Not even the captain was informed of their destination and mission.